# *Forsaking Magic*

# *Forsaking Magic*

Julian Norwood

Marble, NC USA

2014

This is a work of fiction. Names, characters, businesses, places, events and incidents are either the products of the author's imagination or used in a fictitious manner. Any resemblance to actual persons, living or dead, or actual events is purely coincidental.

First Edition 2014

Printed in Charleston, SC USA



Word Branch Publishing
PO Box 474
Marble, NC 28905

http://wordbranch.com
catherine@wordbranch.com

Library of Congress Control Number: On file with publisher

ISBN-13: 978-0692209134
ISBN-10: 0692209131

For Loki, Isaac, and Michelle, thank you for your support.

Special thanks to Victor, who edited this and still talks to me afterward.

And Kevin, thank you for putting up with everything.

## Foreword:

A little more than two years ago, a newly graduated artist from a college I used to teach at approached me about illustrating book covers for Word Branch Publishing. Although I had never had Julian as a student, he came highly recommended from my former colleagues, and his work was impressive. Because we were a start-up company with innovative, but low budget, ideas, I could only pay him with percentages of royalties from the books and the hope that this crazy idea would get off the ground. My to my surprise and delight, he said yes.

Since then we have suffered the ups and downs of the publishing world as we have struggled to make a name for ourselves. Without Julian, Word Branch Publishing would not have the unique and distinctive look it has today. He has become an integral part of Word Branch, and I am very lucky to have him as an illustrator.

When he came to me with a book query, I would have said yes no matter the content or quality. But it was a pleasure to discover that he is as talented and dedicated a writer as he is an artist, and Forsaking Magic is a fist novel to be proud of.

Julian has taken on the most difficult task for a writer: addressing a controversial and emotional subject and framing it in an entertaining, well written story. Forsaking Magic captures the struggles teens often have coming to terms with LGBT identities, but it is also engaging fantasy fiction.

I recommend Forsaking Magic as an essential book for transgender teens and parents. The emotions and situations feel real and the dialog genuine. But even more so, Forsaking Magic is entertaining, readable, and charming with gentle humor, deep friendships, and warm family moments.

Sincerely,

Catherine Rayburn-Trobaugh

Owner of Word Branch Publishing

## Chapter One

I can still remember my first time flying. The wind fluttered my shoelaces and threw my hair back in wild tendrils. I was soaring above the trees, above the clouds as my mom held on tight to me. The world whooshed by below as I for the first time felt the wind in my hair. It was the first sign, the slightest hint that I was somehow special, and a little different. It was the first time I felt like I was actually magical.

My dreams melted into consciousness, without a clear transition, and my body felt oddly large and gangly for my ever-shrinking broomstick until the waking world finally overtook me, and I realized I'm in bed. For a long moment, I felt too big for my little room, until my mind wrapped itself around the scale of things and cleared itself of sleep. I still had the brief, vivid wisps of dream trying to escape my grasp, those moments of taking to the clouds and soaring over everything.

But then… then I looked out my bedroom window and saw the short stretches of grass, and Dad's fenced in vegetable garden, and hedges and flowers all the way to the property border. Everything looked bigger as a kid, and my nostalgia started to fade. I was never a very reliable narrator, and five year old me was even worse. Those old memories of soaring above the trees and through clouds couldn't have been hovering any more than five feet off the ground, zipping around the perimeter of the yard, as Mom held on to me for dear life so I wouldn't fall off. She didn't let me mount up and fly unassisted until I was nine. By the time you're twelve, you realize how tiny your yard is. Anything more than a few feet of a good running start, and I was dodging the fence or the hedges, there wasn't any room for a good straightaway. I used to envy my cousins, because they had a nice farm in Ohio to go zoom around on. Here, I had a half-acre double lot in suburbia that only felt big when it was my turn to mow it.

My ceremonial broom was hung on the back of my door, faded and neglected. It was birch and willow, braided with dried lavender sprigs and long grape vines, an embossed leather strap keeps it fastened to its hook. Occasionally, I had to sweep up bits of leaves and flowers. Sometimes I forgot it was there, and would beat it to death if I opened the door too fast. These days, it was like an old childhood stuffed animal, something I'm almost embarrassed of, that's seen much better days, but I don't know if I'll ever get rid of it. Then again, much like my stuffed animals, I'm not sure Mom would let me anyway. At least I didn't have to hide it away from friends because only one of them was ever over anyway.

The alarm on my phone sprung to life, twittering away the same excessively cheerful chiming that greets me every morning. I picked it up and fiddled with the puzzle of stroking just right to shut it up, and not just lull it to sleep for another five minutes. I got up, and staggered to fumble in my dresser for the day's clothing. I gave up on the art of matching and fashion a long time ago, now it's all cargo pants, cargo shorts, and the occasional pair of slacks for when Dad decides I need to be half-presentable. I don't bother dodging the old witch stereotypes, it's all in black. I won't lie; this had a bit to do with laziness. I hated matching. Besides, it helped me look slimmer, less like I'm all hips and, well, other things my mom calls assets. She says the "Goddess figure" runs in the family. I feel less like a goddess, and more like I'm stuck with the body of a renaissance art model, complete with a big hook nose.

One sports bra later, I feel at least a little less "gifted" and more sleek, or at least more visually balanced as I half-heartedly study myself in my wardrobe mirror. Yes, I have a wardrobe, part of being in a colonial house is the lack of the invention of the closet. I still haven't found Narnia yet. I surveyed myself, standing up tall, slouching, finger-combing my hair. My outfit did nothing to conceal my hips, pants ballooning out my legs in the name of pocket space. I straighten again and lift my chin. My shoulders are what command attention when I stand up straight, and not, well, other nonsense.

Clothing, check. Outside the house next door, I could hear muffled grumbling, and the sound of an engine trying to start up. It's followed immediately by a sound like a gunshot, and a cloud of blue smoke meanders its way across the yard, giving it a temporary mysterious, oil-reeking haze. Right on time. I brushed my hair proper-like, not with fingers, as I listened to the melody of what sounds a lot like a dying lawn mower doing battle with an industrial sewing machine.

William had probably been up for hours at this point. He had hauled his toolbox out of the garage and was half straddling most of a "motorcycle." It was the morning ritual of a process he kept calling restoration, but seemed to me to just be wrenching and screwing things, then doing a lap or two around the block with seemingly no change at all no matter what he did. The last time it looked or sounded different was six months ago when he put a chrome luggage rack on it. He mounted up, tucked in, and was off to go loop-de-loop the block while I half-watched as I brushed my hair. By sound alone, it seemed like our house was being circled by the world's fastest weed whacker.

"Abigail, breakfast!"

Clothing, check. Hair, check. Well, I was more or less ready to start the day. I grabbed my phone and my messenger bag, and headed to the kitchen where my dad was adding half the spice rack to a pot of oatmeal, making the room smell deceptively of pumpkin pie. It was a sweet, heavenly lie of a scent, a delicious tease.

"That's mean."

"What is, hon?" he asked as he ladled it into bowls before he sprinkled on a dash of cinnamon.

"Your oatmeal of deception." I sat heavily, or probably just flopped, and chuckled. It's odd for a teenage girl, I know. I've never really been the giggling sort.

"It's pumpkin pie spice. You like pumpkin pie spice." He set a bowl in front of me. "Have you seen Laurie yet?"

"Nope, can't hear him either." Few things are more suspicious than a quiet five year old. "And I like pumpkin pie, and I like oatmeal, I'm just not sure about your hybrid."

"Trust me, you'll like this," he said as he walked towards my brother's room. Famous last words.

I was usually a good sport about his experiments, and it did smell delicious, for a culinary lie. I had to stick to my principles, though. I had never been a fan of things that act like what they are not, and that included food. I wanted my coffee to taste like coffee, and petty as it sounds, my oatmeal to still taste a bit like oatmeal, and not strange, lumpy, fake pie.

After I sampled, and gave it a rigorous mental critique, I deduced that it is edible, and remembered that I was actually hungry. It wasn't all that bad for being fake pie. I was halfway through the bowl when Dad came back, and my haphazardly dressed brother was half-dragged along. "Morning, Laurie," I said politely, with as much cheer as I can muster. He glared and grumbled, and swung himself into a chair, reaching for my glass of juice. "Nope. Get yet own." I slid it out of his grasp. He shot me the most deadly scowl a chipmunk-faced kindergartener can muster.

"Daaaa-" he started to whine.

"Laurie, get a cup and get some." His eyes widened and he swiftly added, "Not a glass!" I think he remembered the last time he told Laurie to get his own drink, and the glassware went one shelf higher for it.

My brother sighed with all the drama of a seasoned actress and lumbered out of his chair like his butt is made of lead and his knees can't bend. He approached for the fridge with a morose, stiff-legged shuffle. No one inherited my father's morning person genes. Mom was either in bed already or not back from work yet, I hadn't bothered to check if her car was in the driveway when I was getting dressed.

"It's too high!" my brother nearly wailed upon reaching the fridge, after a moment of bouncing and groping at the carton, just out of reach. He started to slam the refrigerator door in protest, and Dad caught it just in time.

"I'll get it; you pour it, and knock it off. Don't wake your mother." He had a knack for a sort of firm cheer I had only ever seen in my father and retail workers. The world's fastest weed eater was approaching, and parked behind our garage after a brief sprint through the snow-covered grass. He didn't crash this time.

"Think William will want some?" My father gestured at the crock of unappreciated oatmeal.

I paused to really ponder it over, touching my chin, giving a loud hmmmm, then spoke,"Is it food?"

He tensed, and looked on the verge of reprimand, then dropped it. He was trying not to smile, "Valid point." He let me get away with a little snark in the mornings, since at least I'm vertical and articulate. Besides, it was a challenge to find food Will wasn't going to try to mooch. He had a knack for showing up at meals, even when he'd already had one earlier, and it was a good way for my father to test things we weren't quite ready for. Mom was sneakier; she had the habit of using him to clean the fridge if he stuck around long enough.

My brother was pacified with juice and breakfast, and we had a few seconds of quiet before Will showed up. He let himself in through the back door, through the garage, like he always did. From the sound of things, he fell up the steps before he staggered in through the door. He did his best to make it look dramatic and intentional as he removed his helmet and straightened his coat.

"Morning Miss, morning Sir," he says to me, then my father, tipping his imaginary hat. He sits next to Laurie and pats his head, "Hey

Truck." It was a nickname I never quite understood, but it had something to do with British slang. Laurie didn't mind the nickname, but he did mind the head-pat and gave a feeble swat, then scrunched up and smoothed down his hair again.

"Morning Will, Want some breakfast? How's the bike holding up this morning?" He didn't have a moment to respond before my father had handed him a bowl, which he took eagerly.

"Well, she's cold blooded, that's for sure. Was a b-bear to start this morning." I held in a chuckle and snort when he stumbled into the word "bear," when another had almost rolled off his tongue. "I bet I can get her almost up to highway speeds come spring, still starts to bog down at forty five, any thoughts?"

"That is a puzzler." My father nodded with a well rehearsed bluff of a wise expression, "Any other…symptoms? "He owned a motorcycle himself, but it was back in the Honda dealership every time it made an ill-timed squeak or didn't spring to life with a turn of the key. I could never recall him working on it himself in a way that wasn't a minor adjustment, but he always spoke with Will like he was a seasoned mechanic. Actually, I think mostly he smiled, nodded, and let Will talk himself out of it. The way he was with his bike was nothing like Will, who'd built it from just a frame and a leaky engine two years ago. Most kids brought puppies home and begged to keep them, Will did that with vehicles.

"Yeah, it could be a few things, but I'm pretty sure I just need to rejet and tweak the carbs, and with luck I don't have to order something else from Italy." Will chattered away between heaping bites of oatmeal.

"You had to pick something so rare, eh fancy boy?" I nudged him with an elbow, and aimed for the ribs.

"It needed me," he drew himself up in a dignified manner and gestured with his spoon, sending a scoop of oatmeal plopping onto his sleeve. He gave it a brief look of disgust, then wiped it off with his fingertip and ate the offending blob. Then he shot me a brief, intense, "You saw nothing." sort of look, and resumed the rather one-sided conversation he was having with my father. Laurie was almost silent; he just stared forlornly at his mostly untouched oatmeal and drained juice.

"I thought it was going to be pie," he announced sadly.

"Me too buddy." I patted his arm knowingly and held in a laugh as I retreated to my room to grab my things for school. I left Dad at the mercy of an over-caffeinated "petrol-head" as he liked to call himself.

"You giving me a ride?" I call down the hall.

"Yeah, sure, just get your helmet and jacket."

"Is the ice cleared up?" my dad asked, voicing his only real concern on the issue.

"Yeah, mostly, but it's f-freaking cold outside." Another linguistic near-miss.

"Take the bus; I don't want you hitting any ice."

"Yessir." I could almost hear him nodding; he always does that when he says sir.

"Abby, hurry up!" he called after me. I grabbed my phone and stuffed my homework into my bag. I tried to stride out looking confident, all shoulders and standing tall, but it went entirely unnoticed My minor effort was soon buried under a red marshmallow coat that could endure any Connecticut winter. Will just tossed his leather pea coat back on and followed me out with backpack in hand. We hadn't left the driveway before he was red in the face and pale in the fingertips, and seemed to pull on his backpack for some false shred of warmth.

"You have got to be cold." I gave him a sideways glance as he hunched under his backpack.

"A dire understatement, my dear, I am freezing my ass off."

Being seventeen and still riding the bus is a great way to be branded with the mark of the loser, part of why I like to tag along with Will as much as possible. It was somehow slightly less nerdy to arrive on a mirror-covered Vespa, at least it showed I have a friend with a ride of some sort, no matter how eccentric said friend of said vehicle happened to be. I leaned on the window and watched the world go by. Just a week ago, it was buried in a blanket of white, and five foot plowed drifts still looming on some corners, with ominous canyons plowed out for sidewalks. That's one way that the memories of things being so big still hold true, a good snowfall around here will make anyone feel four years old again, usually as you're digging out your front door. The last snow fall like this was four years ago, and I remembered my little brother clinging to my hand in mild terror as we walked to the gas station through the snow canyons to buy another cord of firewood and some more marshmallows.

Though I guess all that needs to be said about winter here is that, you can buy fire wood at the gas station. Any gas station.

"We should have flown today," Will said out of the blue. He seemed to have finally thawed.

"By private helicopter or rabbit-shaped catapult?"

"By broom, though I am partial to the catapult idea."

"Broom?" I looked at him like I had no idea what he was talking about.

"We could arrive in style, flying in, gracefully touching down, and you just throw it over your shoulder, and we strut to class. Maybe do a loop-de-loop or barrel roll or something in the process." He gestured in the air while making whooshing noise.

"That sounds… horrifying, actually. I'm pretty sure we would crash and fall to our death."

"Okay, no barrel rolls then, but you know it sounds awesome."

"Yeah, and it's also illegal." I lowered my voice a bit. I didn't want to broadcast my status too loudly, even if it wasn't much of a secret. It was, thankfully, a mostly forgotten trait of mine, like when I took up playing the cello and wanted to be Yo Yo Ma for about eight months.

"Illegal for witches to fly? That's discrimination!" He started to rant before I could even continue, and I shut him up with a well-aimed poke between the ribs. Will yelped, and I felt no remorse.

"Not illegal illegal, but, well, hard to do legally. Now they make you have a pilot's license, and a working radio on you, and you're supposed to only take off and land at airfields and be over and under certain heights. You can only really just zoom all over and have fun on your own property, and even then, it has to be under forty feet and not too close to a military base." It was a common subject for my mother to go off on, ever since she finally gave up and had to stay grounded in the early eighties. She had even logged a fair number of flight training hours before the rules changed again. "Now they're pushing for safety gear and such."

"On a broom?" he said, staring at me in disbelief.

"Yep. For your own good."

"Is that why you don't do it anymore?"

"Kind of. Can't really do much in the yard, not allowed on the street, there's only so many times you really enjoy blasting over the house, you know." I shrugged, "Mom says I should start taking Laurie for rides, since she doesn't get up until later."

"Why not just teach him how to do it?" He grinned at me. "I bet that would be hilarious."

"Boys can't fly, Will, remember?"

"Oh, yeah." He leaned back on the bench as best as he could, half-curling to prop his knees on the front of it.

"Boy witches can't fly, girl weres can't shift, and well, I'm sure the rest have their own oddities too."

"Your genes are sexist."

"So are yours, bunny-boy."

## Chapter Two

When I met William, I was utterly smitten. I was head-over heels, loved him, and wanted to take him home with me and keep him forever. But eventually, he turned back into a five year old boy when I had liked him much better as a rabbit.

I didn't know what a "were" was at the time, aside from a passing pop-culture knowledge of the most majestic, fierce, and frequently faked of them all, the were-wolf. William didn't get that lucky, he didn't even have the luck of being a were-bear, or were-stag, like his father.

We met in the garden in autumn, when he had escaped his home and gone foraging. He was fast. I was faster, and I knew the lay of the garden, and by a stroke of dumb luck, also managed to trap him under a pail. I proudly came dragging home fifteen pounds of squirming, kicking hare, begging to keep him and promising everything little kids do when they want a new pet. Offer a child a pet, and they will turn into saints in order to get it. I was going to love him, pet him, feed him, brush him, go on adventures with him, and do everything aside from keep him in a pen and promptly forget I had him, like the hamster that later became my mother's hamster.

But, my father had a hunch he belonged to someone, he was no eastern cottontail. Thankfully, he turned back before we turned him over to animal control. I wasn't exactly pleased when the dream bunny I swore I had always wanted forever turned into a crying little boy. Actually, I'm pretty sure I punched him in the arm and told him that he was a cry baby, and that I hated him because he took the rabbit away, and then my mother sent me to my room.

It's not how friendships usually start, but it worked well enough. It also gave my parents something they needed, another family of weirdoes to connected with. I was almost as common a fixture at William's house as he was at mine. His home tended to be much more crowded on any given day, with at least six children present at any point in time, give or take friends being over, or a few being away. They were all largely free-range, the house rules "be back before the street lights come on" or "If you miss dinner, you aren't getting it." There were always people coming and going and a constant drone of chatter that always felt like it was just coming out of the walls.

I think it was for this reason that Will lived in the garage. He would tinker with his scooter, or his parents' cars, or his brother's on occasion whenever it needed something ridiculous done to it, or needed saving from something ridiculous having been done wrong. Knocking twice on the garage door, it lazily began to rise with a mechanical clunking, and I found William in his natural habitat.

"Still trying to get it on the highway?" I asked, sitting on a picnic bench that's been moved inside for the season. I lay back, on it, and lazily dug thorough my bag for my Gameboy. It was the old, yellow brick in all its green screened glory.

"No, my exhaust fell off." He peeked out from around his scooter, practically hugging it with his legs and surrounded by bits and pieces of it.

"How did you manage that?" I loaded up a cartridge and never really looked his way.

"Magic, gremlins, who knows. I'm starting to think this thing's cursed, it's always breaking. I mean, there's classic European engineering, and then there's 'I'm pretty sure someone cursed this.'"

"Classic European engineering?" I looked up a moment and arched my brow as much as I could.

"Old European vehicles break, a lot, it's part of the charm and part of what kind of makes it a hobby. Like, Citroën's are where the term "lemon" came from for a car, and any LBC—"

"LBC?" I sigh, "More terminology. Less techno babble."

"It's an acronym, not techno babble." He looked down his nose at me and held up a finger, "It means Little British Car or convertible. They leak oil everywhere and have electrical gremlins that you haven't seen since World War II."

"So why own one?"

"Because it's a project, it gives you something to do and keep busy with."

"Isn't that why you're mad at it?"

"Shut it." He sighed, and looks up at me, "Honestly, it wouldn't be so bad if I didn't have to order the parts from the U.K. and Italy."

"So why do you have it?"

"Because it's cool."

"I don't believe you. I haven't seen anyone on one of those things—"

"Well, they were cool, back in the 60s, you know, mod culture and such." He backed down for a rare moment, "I still think they're cool."

"You like everything from back then."

"Damn straight. Classic Doctor Who or MTV, pick one."

"Can we laugh at the cheesy effects?" I asked after what seems like a long moment of severe contemplation. The worried look on his face was priceless; like he was terrified I would choose Snooki over watching the cybermen invade.

"Of course you can." He snapped back to his usual, slightly dignified look.

"Hmm, I'd say that's a winner right there."

When I glanced back up, I find myself staring up his chest, at the underside of his chin, as he watches my screen. He was unnervingly sneaky for being so damned tall. He smirked, and looked down at me, "And you make fun of me for liking old things?"

"At least mine works." I gave the trusty yellow brick a firm pat.

"Touché. By the way, Samus is a girl."

I sighed and shifted a bit, feeling vaguely uncomfortable for a moment, for reasons I wasn't sure I could place. "Yeah, I know. I learned that the first time I beat it."

"Thank you for playing, please enjoy this scantily clad 15 pixel high woman. Please play again, but faster and better, to see her with less clothing," he said in his best announcer voice. I laughed and considered hitting him with it at the same time. The door into the house opened suddenly, and we were both stunned silent and left staring blankly at it, like deer in headlights. In his case, maybe it was more like a stunned rabbit.

"William, degrease and come— Oh, hey Abby." His older brother stood in the doorway, taking up most of it. He was the tall and athletic, a track and basketball kind of guy. His features were sharp, but not quite in the bird-ish way that William seems stuck with, and not quite as tan, with copper-brown hair. If I didn't know the spectrum of siblings in between, I wouldn't think them related.

Despite his active sports background and moderate popularity around school, he magically managed to not be completely insufferable to be around. He even had his moments of being less obnoxious than Will.

"Hey, bro," I said back, and he gave me a quizzical look before he looked down at his brother.

"Mom needs help with dinner. You're on onion duty, bro." Oh, evidently only he could say bro. He grinned just a bit with a blatant "better you than me" look on his face, which vanished when he looked my way. "You staying for dinner? It's, um…well, actually it's one of Mom's recipes." This often had the same implications as being one of my father's experiments, except for in this case, it was probably very strange or very English, as opposed to the spur-the-moment fusion cuisine my dad was infamous for.

"No thanks." I sat up and backtracked on my game to a save spot, from the days when you couldn't save as you please.

"Wise move," he chuckled as Will washed up in the double sink, filling the air with the smell of oranges as he scrubbed down. He's changed, suddenly quiet and stiff as he hunched over the sink and was deeply focused upon his hands. He was on edge and upset, for reasons I couldn't quite place. Could he really be so annoyed over being pulled from his project? I was trapped until I found a checkpoint and powered down my game. When I closed my eyes, I felt the tension prickling in the air. My skin started to crawl when I find myself focusing on it. I broke free and shook the sensation away.

"Gonna be by later tonight, bunny boy?" I asked as I casually tossed the brick into my bag. He gave an ambiguous noise and shrugs a shoulder, something I've long since learned to mean maybe. "Yeah, well, I'll save you a taco if you do." He disappeared into the house, and I was left to turn off the lights and shut the garage door, shuffling back to my own place. I could feel the energy running under my skin, tiny waves and zig-zags. I could almost trace them with my hand, but I found myself just trying to forcibly rub them away, it was like squeezing a sheet of invisible water off my skin.

I returned home, reeking of gasoline and engine oil just by sharing the same space as Will's project. I undressed in my room and grabbed a robe, still anxious. I didn't feel my mind settle until the shower is running over me, bathroom swiftly becoming a foggy haze. I remembered and then ignored some electricity safety video I still recall from first grade, and stretch to turn off the light with a damp hand. Still and alone in the dark, I felt the water run over me, over every awkward and barely tolerated inch. I started to count. It was slow and meditative, imagining the shape and sound of each number, letting my mind make calligraphic strokes as it went, sweeping brush strokes to find my center again. The din of water made the perfect silence, an organic kind of static. Forty nine morphs and arches along into fifty, with big, open curling patterns that spiral away on me.

"Fifty one." I felt the long swooping curve and then the almost grating single, straight line, and I realize the distress has passed. I still wasn't sure what Will's problem was. I wished it didn't have to bleed over like this, not without good reason. Maybe I won't save him that taco after all. I was a mess all because of his pouting, stupid empathy. There was a knock at the door, and my eyes snapped open.

"Abby? Honey, you okay?" I jumped a bit upon hearing my mother's voice. Usually I showered at night when I could indulgently hog and reign over the bathroom until the hot water ran frigid.

"Yeah, I think I got gas on me or something-" She didn't buy that, I knew she didn't, and I quickly added, "And I got a bad aura, that's all." She understood, she's been there too. She often reminded me that things are at their most intense when you're young, and you don't know how to quite cope. I try, anyway. I had my numbers, my mental calligraphy. It got the job done, and I was now more annoyed at Will than anything, even if I didn't really have good reason. I know I don't, I know I couldn't control his thoughts, he still clammed up on me like that, and his aura was so sharp and prickling like ice water and—

I shudder under the water, and struggled to remembered twenty six, and let my mind spirals again into a pastoral field of curls.

"Abby?" She knocked more urgently.

"I'm all right." I forced my voice calm, "Be out in a second."

"I'll go light some sage for you and get some tea…" It hadn't ever done much good, but I think it makes her feel like she can help. I don't actually like tea, especially the strong, black, punchy sort with lemon she always brings, but the warmth of the gesture is calming in itself. Though sometimes, the smell of sage would remind me of one of Dad's cooking experiments, gone up in smoke.

"Okay Mom, thanks…"

I threw on my robe before I hit the light, avoiding every mirror I could until I was safe in my room. Even the brief glimpse I saw of myself felt wrong, but right now, everything was wrong. Stupid Will. Stupid empathy. Stupid body.

I hated when it happened. My mother told me, after calming down a past panic that it was a defense mechanism and that could help me stay away from trouble. Eventually, she just relented and said it ran in the family, and tried to convince me that it had its perks. I didn't believe that for a moment. I hadn't seen any "perks," not then, not now, it just made the world feel more intense. I knew every time Will started sulking, or my parents tried to fight quietly in their bedroom. I even knew Laurie's seemingly inconsolable pain and sorrow when he threw tantrums when he was a toddler, because I felt it right along with him. I would meditate where I could, to learn how to drown it out. I didn't want to feel the pain of everyone around me just because we happened to be in close proximity. Grade seven had been hell, as everyone's insecurities had burrowed into my skull. Thankfully, I wasn't in seventh grade anymore, and it gotten better, a lot better, but sometimes I was caught off guard.

I was still considering whether or not I'd save Will a taco when a nap snuck up on me, and the waking world faded away into flying dreams. I could go so high…

## Chapter Three

I was thirteen when we had my coming of age party. It was at my grandmother's house in Ohio. Family came from miles around, we had a big bonfire in the country, and it was all in my honor. It meant that I was finally a real witch, that I could start training in a craft if I chose it. I thought mostly that it was an excuse to get everyone together and have a little fun. The actual ritual was brief, I was presented with my ceremonial broom, my grandmother said a prayer over me, my mother cried, and everyone chattered about how grown up and beautiful I had become. Truthfully, what I recall most was pelting full-blast through the woods, chasing my cousins and frightening squirrels, as the food took center stage back at the party. Formality and ritual was the last thing on anyone's mind, as the comforts of food and family seemed to be a longer running tradition for us all. It was a chance to get together, celebrate, and eat. I still remember the cake most of all.

I leaned back in the car and watched Pennsylvania slowly go by. It faded from the erratic, snowy hills of Connecticut with its petite so called mountains and thick stone-wall bordered woods, as it gave over to rolling hills dotted with farms that probably looked fresh off a butter label in the spring. The farms were shoved aside by the mountains as we hit the middle of the state. My brother had his nose so firmly wedged against my mother's tablet that I was pretty sure it had to be registering as a third finger. Who knows, maybe he was using it to help fire those colorful birds across the screen. They made cute noises four hours ago, then they seemed to turn to little screams and mocking laughter as they became chattering little maniacs leading the charge. I preferred to watch the world go by with the occasional antique session of Quix or good old Pokémon Red. The save function still worked by sheer miracle, and I had passed through Lavender Town when we hit the Ohio border. We drove into the setting sun, on our way to my little cousin's coming of age party. Something told me this was going to be a more festive affair. It wasn't hard to imagine since Victoria, the queen of magenta, was the lady of the hour.

The essence of Ohio hit like a well-flung brick, as the mountains stopped abruptly and gave way to a sea of empty farm fields, which would be an abyss of corn in the summer. As we went south, we flirted with the foothills, but couldn't escape the agriculture until we were almost at our destination. Our car retreated into the safety of the woods, like it was finally back where it belonged again. The pixelated birds weren't the only thing angry anymore; Laurie had been wiggling impatiently for almost an hour. He swapped through every electronic means of entertainment within reach, including a brief session on my Gameboy which he proclaimed to be too hard.

"Look out the window for a while," my dad suggested as he was once more jarred from the nap he could never quite manage to take.

"It's dark." said Laurie glumly.

"Then look at the lights."

He'd been in the passenger seat for three hours with his eyes shut as Mom drove, and he stirred at every electronic boop or pulled headphone jack that left the car stuck hearing three seconds of a heavy metal cover of "O Fortuna." I blamed Laurie for that one. I said his foot caught the cord, but it was really all my doing.

We pulled up to my great-aunt's house, formerly my grandmother's home. The gravel lot was packed tight, and the only lights in sight were the stars above, and the warm glow from within the house. It was like a giant lantern, as golden light poured from every tall, colonial window. I could hear the low murmur of talk even outside, once our car was off, it was the only noise. Normally the air would be full of frogs, crickets and night birds, but they were all tucked away for the winter.

We grabbed our bags from the trunk, and headed for the house, and I felt a mixed sense of excitement and dread as I was suddenly immersed in a swarm of tightly cramped relatives.

It was a blur of hugs and kisses and tightly squeezed hands as I found my clothes now swimming in a mix of everyone's perfumes. I was hit with everything from "You're getting so big," to "You're looking just like your mother did at your age." I even got a "Does your mother honestly let you dress like that?" as my aunt looked me over in my cargo pants and obscure Celtic-rock T-shirt. Laurie got the brunt of the greeting and cooing, he'd been three and a half last time most of the family had seen him, and unlike me, he had actually grown. I weaved through the crowd, giving my polite hellos along the way to a lot of family I had barely met, and managed to squeeze into the kitchen. At least there, I could graze on what was left of the spread. By now, it was mostly deviled eggs and cold casseroles, but I managed to steal some ham and find a quiet corner. I felt adrift, lost at sea. No one here really knew me, they just thought they did, when what they were remembering was eight year old me, or baby me. Teenage me was harder nut to crack.

My phone buzzed after the fourth time that I was asked how school was, a question I never quite learned how to respond to, thankfully my mother swooped in to brag for me. I was grateful for a way out, but found it was just a text message instead of a call. Actually, it was a lot of text messages, but mostly all the same. Will was bored without me. I played antisocial from the crowd, finding a real sense of familiarity in talking with my best friend, even if we talked mostly in parroted memes and in-jokes peppered with creative emoticons. I couldn't remember feeling this out of place among family before, like I was a weird creature that wasn't quite the same species as the children running hyperactive laps around furniture. The middle-aged talked of children and recent family gossip, while one of the only real familiar faces, a cousin who was two years older than me, was talking to one of my aunts while holding a brand new baby.

I did the math in my head and shuddered. I always knew that sort of thing could happen, but it was unsettling to see my old favorite cousin as now being a part of her own family unit. She didn't go to college, go travel Europe, or go on all those adventures we used to talk about. Wife, husband, and baby makes three, and the idea made me retreat back into the written word, breaking away from our fifteen minute spree of sending each other funny pictures.

**[My cousin bred.}** I wrote to him, and waited for the signal to catch up, as his first response seemed to be a picture of a parakeet, which had nothing to do with the conversation at all.

**{Baby Bred?]**

**[Yep}**

**{Ew.]**

I let out a loud and snorting laugh at what had to look like nothing at all. "Heh, talking to a friend." I gestured down at my phone, so no one assumed I found the deviled eggs to be quite that interesting.

"Abby, go socialize." My mother sighed as she went through the meager pickings the buffet still had to offer.

"I did Mom."

"Go actually socialize."

"About what? There's nothing to talk about."

"School, or your friends, and you haven't told anyone about that award you got for your photography. I'm sure you can find something to talk about."

I sighed loudly, and that was a mistake. Her voice had been cheerful and encouraging, but then I actually met her gaze. She gave me the look that said that I was embarrassing her, as she rolled her eyes slightly then glared from behind the frame of chestnut hair and silver glasses that seemed to bracket the intensity of her expressions. It was all in the eyes with her.

"Yes Mom," I made sure to drain anything that could be seen as sarcasm out of those words, and wondered if it's too weird to call your own mother ma'am. I pocketed the phone, and headed back out into the crowd with my plate.

"Abby!" My cousin called to me while waving with her free hand as her baby stared doe-eyed at everything and nothing all at once. It was in a sling now, something I had only ever seen on hippy parents at the farmer's market, and I had trouble wrapping my head around my cousin in one.

"Hi Sylvia," I tried to say with as much genuine enthusiasm as I could, while I attempted to swallow half an egg at once. After a moment's hesitation, I headed over to greet her, weaving around an uncle and a tall brass lamp.

"How are things?" She smiled at me, so genuine and bubbly, almost bouncing in place.

"Good. I won an award in photography." Then I remembered she didn't ask how school went, and I felt as socially capable as ever. Nice job, Abby. "I— My mom made me say that. Things are… good." I was as articulate and eloquent as I had been all evening.

"Want to hold Brynn? You two haven't met yet have you?" She laughed then smiled down at the perpetually-startled looking baby in her arms.

"You know I'd love to but I have this—" I gesture at my plate.

"Well you can set it down here." She smiles at me, and I'm hit with a wave of dread. Crap. I froze like a deer on a freeway as I tried to remember how to hold a baby, or even what to do with a baby. I choked and wondered if Brynn was a boy or a girl, and realized it was probably too late to just ask politely at this point. I reluctantly set my plate aside, and accepted the slightly lop-sided and ever so slightly moving child. All

I could remember at that moment was to support the head and don't drop it.

"Hi Brynn," I cracked a timid smile down at the little human in my arms and was met with the same wide-eyed and confused stare that Brynn seemed to use on everything. Well, at least we had something in common.

"See? She likes you," said Sylvia.

I resisted the urge to ask how she could tell. I thought maybe she could read Brynn's aura. Maybe she had a psychic connection, or maybe that was just the polite thing to say if you hand someone a baby and it doesn't start screaming. I was thankful that Brynn hadn't started screaming but just continued to look doe-eyed and profoundly confused. I wondered if she ever blinked.

Sylvia grinned ear to ear, it was like the act of me holding her was lighting up her very soul. I was just happy she had revealed Brynn's gender to me, without having to awkwardly dance around avoiding a single pronoun. I wondered how long I should hold her, and if Sylvia would be offended if I handed her back. It was hard to think of anything to say other than "Yep, yep, that's definitely a nice baby you have there," so I settled for the thing I usually said when someone introduced me to their new puppy.

"She's really cute," I said, forcing an awkward smile.

"Thanks, she looks a lot like her dad, but I'm hoping her hair will darken with age. I was a blonde too when I was little."

So was I, now that I thought about it. It had gone dark just before middle school.

"You have no idea what to do with a baby, do you?" A hint of a sly grin had formed on Sylvia's face, and I was catching a trace of the devious personality I had known and loved.

"Nope, not a bit," I said, looking down at Brynn, who looked up at me. Her expression was still that of profound confusion, and I wondered if that was her default. Sylvia laughed, more heartily than just the polite giggle of amused company. She was finally showing her true colors again, the Sylvia I had remembered from years ago who turned a squirrel loose in my dad's car. "So, does she actually like me?" I asked as I glanced down at Brynn.

"Well, she's not upset by you, she's just kind of…kind of that warm, bubbly feeling you get when you read someone really relaxed." She gestured in the air, fingers waggling.

"She looks…deeply confused."

"So do you."

"And her eyes are so big…"

"Her dad is a stag."

"A were, or are we a priestess of Herne these days?"

And in a flurry of bad innuendos and sarcastic digs, I had my favorite cousin back, even if she did have a plus one. A few years had changed a lot, she was married, in school part time, living in Virginia, and thankfully, she had not yet turned into a mombie.

"Mombie, eh? I like it." She did her best to wall her eyes and go slack jawed. "Isn't my…baby…cute…" she said in a similar way that the shuffling masses would say "brains."

"But you aren't one," I said, all too relieved by this.

"Nah, not yet any way, it might be contagious. I love her, more than anything, but hey, you'll know that someday too huh?"

I suddenly got that weird, disconnected feeling. It was like every day when I got dressed, or when my mother told me how pretty I looked, or when my aunt took a shot at my clothes. It was sudden, deep, like being dumped in the middle of the ocean, while my body stayed behind. It was pure disconnection. It was profoundly wrong.

"Abby? Ground control to Abby. Abby, come in Abby," said Sylvia.

I had forgotten this was no place to hide an emotion, and she looked deeply concerned as I tried my best to rebound back into conversation. Sometimes you had to be careful, it wasn't hard to make loop out of stress, worry, or even anger if two sensitive witches were in a conversation. She pulled out of her worried rut, probably thinking of cute kittens or parakeets running on tightropes or balancing on tennis balls. Then I remembered that that was what I did. She was probably thinking of Brynn.

"No kids for you, huh?"

"N-no, college first. Then, maybe, I don't know." I shrugged it off. She had given me an excellent way out, anyway. "Can you take her back for a second, I'm going to go see if there's still any Dew." I awkwardly passed off the unevenly weighted bundle and went for the kitchen as discretely as I could. I could feel the passing glances as I had undoubtedly just polluted the warm buzz of good feelings in the air as I passed by. Being in a sour mood in a room full of witches always made me feel like there was a rotting fish stuck to my back in a room that smelled of vanilla and chai tea. I had just made it to the drink table when I felt someone hovering behind me. I turned to see my mother, her expression placid, but eyebrows arched in a way that worried me a little.

"Is everything all right?" It was hard to place just what kind of concern she had in her voice, and it made me feel a little scolded.

"Yes, I'm fine." I said rigidly, pulling myself up a bit taller as I poured another red plastic cup of soda.

"All right. I just got worried."

"You don't have to read me like that all the time."

"You're my daughter; I can do it whenever I think I need to." I heard her voice tighten, and I decided to drop the subject. There was no way I could argue it. I just liked my privacy, what little of it I could have with a witch mom. It was like she was always reading my hypothetical diary. There was a long pause as I tried to sip my soda with dignity and not start a confrontation, and for once, I was thankful that she did read me. That, or she could just simply smell my fear, because she backed off. "I'm going to put Laurie to bed soon. It's late."

"What are the sleeping arrangements?" I was grateful for a subject change.

"Laurie is with his cousins. Your father and I are on the sofa in the basement to keep an eye on them." They always packed the kids into the basement, and sending my mother as their guardian was like tasking a German shepherd with a herd of guinea pigs; sheer overkill and likely to end in barking, squealing, and someone being terrified to death.

"So where am I? Down with the micros?"

"You're with Sylvia and Taylor."

"Doesn't Sylvia get her own married room or something?"

"Her husband's not here, and she wanted to catch up with you and Taylor. Enjoy your time together; you don't get to talk much to your family." Given how most of my night had gone, I wondered if there might be a reason for that. "You'll be in Grandma's old sewing room."

The party quieted down once the kids were herded off to bed in clusters. My father had excused himself to go keep an eye on things, and Sylvia had vanished to probably do something with Brynn. And I was left in a room of people I had no connection with at all.

It looked like most of the teenage boys in the family had escaped off somewhere, and I wished I could have escaped with them. I could have at least listened to them talk in circles about cars they didn't really understand, or argue about the latest "humans shooting things" games, which I was practically an expert on. At least there would be a little common ground, and I nearly regretted not seeking them out earlier when I had been sulking around the buffet.

I decided to go congratulate the lady of the hour, since it seemed polite and she was otherwise the only one even half as close to my age.

She was still up, her mother anxiously hovered nearby to soak up any residual praise or compliments she could, always quick to chime in about how she had made her dress, broom, and daughter completely perfect. My little cousin carried herself like a queen, with ribbons always artfully braided into her hair, and perfect posture that would have made my spine crackle had I straightened like that. Victoria thrived on attention, though even she seemed to be getting tired of being asked how school was going, especially since every time her mother had to butt in about how she was on honor roll or somehow taking honors courses in middle school.

"Hey Vic, big day tomorrow huh?" It was only after I started talking that I realized I had no idea how to actually handle this. I didn't know what to say, and congratulations on surviving to thirteen seemed sarcastic.

"Yes, quite. I'm very excited." She shot me a Stepford wife's smile with remarkable accuracy for a thirteen year old.

"Got a dress picked out?" I figured she had been asked this a dozen times, but it was better than "How's school?"

"Yes, it's—" And my aunt swooped in, eager to describe it in painstaking detail that I didn't really understand. I had never sewn an anything, that was something my aunts and Sylvia liked to do. Hell that was something William could do better than I could, though he claimed it was upholstering and a vital manly skill.

"Neat." I nodded and looked more vacant than I intended to.

"Have you been accepted into college yet?" asked Victoria, who had obviously trained better for this conversation than I had, "Or will you be pursuing a traditional studies program?"

"Well, I'm seventeen; I have another year for that." I knew I should have been planning this a while ago.

"I see. I plan to attend a traditional studies program in healing or seeking when I turn sixteen, and then from there I plan to attend Miami

University, and then—" I realized she had all of this planned far better than I, or maybe it was her mother talking for her, and she was just a very well trained parakeet of a child.

"Wow, that's great." I had just been utterly shown up by an almost thirteen year old. I hadn't even paid any thought to a traditional studies program; I had no intention of going off on the path witches had for years. I had barely even considered college, aside from knowing that it was probably a good idea. This kid had her entire life planned out and ready to go, and I wasn't sure if I was intimidated by her or just unnerved. And then I could tell the little brat was reading me, because her perky, confident smile turned into a smug little reptilian smirk.

"Well, good luck Abigail, with whatever you finally decide to do."

"Yeah, you too." I excused myself from the conversation, seeking out my grandmother's sewing room in a rush. The last thing I needed to hear was to be asked how school was, because now I didn't have a clue. Good grades and the ability to take a semi-decent photo, that was all I had going for me, and that was crap right now. I retreated to the room, shutting the door behind me. My bags had found their way up on their own, and I had already sent William a text when I looked up and caught my cousin with her shirt open, her daughter cradled in her arm as she nursed.

I unrolled my sleeping bag, Syl had the bed, and Brynn in a nearby folding bassinet. I didn't even know they made those. I tried my best to look at anything but her; I had never quite known how to handle such a situation. I didn't know if I could start talking to her, or look at her, or if I was looking ridiculous by trying to do everything but look at or talk to her.

"You're freaking out again, aren't you?" she asked. I froze up, and then nodded.

"Yeah, I'm good at that tonight."

"You sure are." She nodded in agreement.

"I'm going to go change." I had more or less set up camp for the night, with my dark blue pillow and my mismatched olive mummy bag, my faithful camping companion.

"Why not here? Who knows what the bathroom line is like." She wrinkled her nose a bit.

"I can wait." I gathered up my "pajamas" which were in fact just an old shirt and part of hole-riddled cargo shorts. I discovered she was right, there was a line, and I brushed my teeth at record speed and dressed, met with an odd look or two as I retreated to the sewing room in what looked more like painting clothes than PJs.

"Those are you—"

"Yup." I nodded after making a very pondering face.

"Don't own any?"

"Nope."

"And that's why I brought Yoga pants."

We talked ourselves to sleep, catching up, and feeling that spark of what made us friends in the first place. You can't pick your family, but I could choose who to let into my world.

# Chapter Four

When I woke the next morning, I realized my cousin Taylor had joined us sometime after I had nodded off. She was on an air mattress in a blue sleeping bag, and I was amazed that I had somehow missed hearing her inflate it or drag it in. Everyone was still asleep, even Brynn, and I savored the first real moment of quiet since I had arrived. I missed waking to the sound of the world's fastest weed whacker, to the smell of my father cooking, or the obnoxious clatter of William's tool box on wheels as it was pushed down his driveway every day, stiff wheel and all.

I was waking up on a different planet. One full of witches and magic and family and the essence of Ohio. I found myself missing planet Connecticut, with neighborhood rabbit boys, feet upon feet of snow, and twenty year old cartridge games in my best friend's garage. I looked up at the walls of the "sewing room," which it was only on technicality since it did contain a sewing machine. It had functioned more as my grandmother's den, and the walls were covered in memorabilia, trophies from the past, and things picked up on travels near and far. Fading sepia faces smiled across the room at each other from aging photographs, everything from old sweethearts who signed their names and left love notes on the back, to pictures of planes with cockily grinning pilots with lines like "Thanks for the escort" and a reminder of where he might be next. A newspaper clipping showed a cluster of coyly smiling witches, posed mounted up on their brooms in military uniform with pointy hats on their head for the photo-op. My favorite, though, was a blurry shot out the window of a plane, because there she was, tucked in tight like a jockey in a race, earphones and a balaclava flattening back her hair, as my twenty year old grandmother flew escort. The story below was what made it fantastic. She'd saved their lives, carrying just a blinking beacon in a storm, taking them back to base. The photo was of course, unrelated, it was a sunny day as she was guiding a pilot in training, but every time I visited, I begged her to read me the story.

Now that I could read, I realized she might have embellished a few things, as I was quite sure she wouldn't be carrying a flashing light over enemy territory for over a hundred miles. Sometimes I wished I had never actually read the story, because her version was much, much cooler. She could spin a tale better than any man who had ever fished. It was surreal to me to remember that now, she was away in a nursing home, when the woman I had heard everything about was someone who risked being killed by a propeller every day for fifteen years.

Taylor shifted and let out a single, roaring snore as she rolled over. Even in her sleep, her hair was still unusually well kept. I wondered if she had put a spell on it, or if the magic was in the bulging shower bag that sat on top of her rolling periwinkle and cream, suitcase, which matched her sleeping bag, and her pillow. It was a level of color coordination that seemed alien to me, like she must have ferreted around a store with swatches and a magnifying glass. The snore woke Brynn, who burbled and cooed in her bassinet.

I was adrift in a sea of estrogen, in my ratty cargo shorts and Beatles shirt. My phone buzzed as it began to slowly migrate itself across the floor. I picked it up, already knowing who else would be up at this hour.

**{Wake up]**

I was right; William was once more up way too early for anyone his age.

**[Sleeping, go away.}**

I set the phone on my chest. It inched down chest and slid off the hump that wasn't usually there. I was reminded that I had worn my sports bra all night, and hadn't quite put two and two together as to why my shoulders were aching. It would be on another day at least, I had only brought that.

**{No you aren't.]**

He even included the apostrophe. He texted like an English teacher. We were solitary early birds, a little too grown-up for our age, but a little too immature at the same time. It felt like we were on a different track entirely from most people our age, and right now I felt literally in between where destiny should be pulling. To one side was the earth mother, who was studying the traditions of our craft, and raising a family, and going to college all at once. To my other side was the living doll without the foggiest idea as to where she was going. I didn't know that for sure, I just assumed based on my past experiences with Taylor, and her unnervingly matched luggage set. She had never been terribly bright in my experience, but made up for it in personality. She was not abysmally dense, but any college without the word "community" in it didn't seem likely to me.

"Don't be a jerk," I almost silently reminded myself, since I had technically not spoken to her at all this year. It was a bad habit I had not been able to shake. I was a judgmental little jerk. My father said that all teenagers had superiority and inferiority issues, and that that's what made us all a little loony. He assured me I would grow out of it, but as I had passed sixteen by and was pushing towards the legal status of adult, I was getting concerned. Technically, I was ten months away from adulthood, and I was still very lost.

**{Wake up.]**

William wasn't dropping it this morning. After a minute or so, my phone began its dance again.

**{It snowed.]**

**[Pics Plz?}**

**{Say it for real.]**

**[Pardon me kind sir but could I trouble you for a photograph of the weather?}**

My smart-assery was rewarded with a photo of a fresh coat of white on what had been dust-ridden piles outside. I sat up enough to look out the second story window of the sewing room, and took a picture of the view outside. It was a spectrum of grey, from naked trees to dead grass, and patches of dirt where grass did not grow, and the gravel of the solitary driveway.

**{Mine's better.]**

**[Bet you can't ride.}**

**{Touché.]**

I wondered for a moment how he got the accent to show up on his phone. The life of the house was slowly unfurling, as little noises became larger, which started to grow and multiply. The over-stuffed house was coming alive again, as adults got coffee and the micros acted like they had already had it, as the noise level began to grow. Brynn squeaked and babbled softly, the energy seemed to be contagious. She was soon awake and wiggling, as her little noises became louder and started to work into a cry. Thankfully, we were spared that moment, as her impatience had woken her mother. I slipped off to change again so that Sylvia could handle baby things. It was a special day, and I changed into the clothes I wore when we occasionally attended Sunday Services, but with a little extra color in my blue button-down shirt and argyle socks. I surveyed myself in the mirror and felt more like I was ready for a funeral than the party that would happen later today, but I was now trapped with my fashion choices. The buttons parted a bit much on my chest than I liked, and I tried to flatten it back down and adjust, as that disconnect started to well up again. It was a strange feeling that something was distinctly not right, like I wasn't quite where I should be. There was a pounding knock on the door by a very small fist, "Gotta go potty!" and my bathroom time was up. It would have to do.

I rummaged in my grandmother's sewing basket for a pin I could use. I eventually gave up and sought out my father, who was practically curled around his cup of coffee that morning, leaning on the porch rail outside despite the cold.

"Can you fix this?" I asked a bit too urgently, holding up the pin.

"What, Pumpkin? Lose a button?" He half-glanced over at me.

"No, my shirt's too small." He took a sip from his mug and looked down, giving my blouse a surgeon's stare. I could see him dissecting the problem and putting it back together in his head. "Yeah, go upstairs, and find a thread that matches, we can fix this."

I was suddenly very thankful for the fact that he was raised in a gaggle of girls, the only son of seven. He'd picked up tools of the trade that my mother wasn't patient enough to learn. My shirt was soon operated on and in recovery, as he showed me how to iron it correctly, all while we danced around my still sleeping cousin on her air mattress.

"Try it now." He turned while I did a quick change, reading one of my grandma's stories of heroism or maybe he was counting the pictures of her admirers, like I sometimes did. I looked down, and moved my arms around a bit. "Success!"

"Good, and next time, try it on before you pack it." He seemed more amused than annoyed, but a fresh cup of coffee called him back downstairs.

"Your dad is awesome," said Sylvia.

"Yeah, I guess so. He makes a pretty good mom."

"That's cool, though. Bucking the gender trends and doing what he likes." I felt a twinge of judgment bubbling up in me. The skirt-wearing eighteen year old with the husband and baby who was studying the most feminine of arts in our family was talking about how awesome it was to screw gender roles. I pushed it aside; I didn't need to think that about the person who felt like my only ally here. I was just being bitter again, for no reason at all, and I instantly felt ashamed for it. I was glad she wasn't reading me, and I tried to pull myself back up out of my moment of self-loathing. "Breakfast looked about done," I remarked, anxious to change the subject and avoid making an almost-accidental dig at the skirt-wearing, baby toting earth mother.

"Sounds good. You look like you need coffee."

"I've been up for over an hour."

"My point still stands, grumpy-butt." And I followed her down with the ever-attached Brynn. I was almost getting fond of her; it felt like she was Sylvia's familiar.

I was definitely not parenting material.

## Chapter Five

I milled around the yard, kicking at stones as I waited for something to happen. My trusty old camera hung around my neck, from an old leather strap I got at the army surplus store. It was hard for me to get into the swing of the "party," especially when I had spent the last three hours helping set up for it. I shouldn't have dressed for it so soon, especially if I would have known my job would be moving and unfolding tables. The garage and part of the driveway was turned into an area to sit and eat, a fire roaring in the garage's wood stove so we'd not all freeze. My uncle's Triumph convertible was sitting in the lot with the rest of the cars, for once not under a cover and hiding in the garage. I wondered if it had ever had gravel under its wheels before, let alone in a light dusting of snow. I snapped a picture for William.

I was called away from my thoughts to help put the food out. I was a little jealous, she got a fancy cake for her party, airbrushed with a witch on a broom and a sparkling night's sky, with what I hoped was edible glitter, and her name in fancy script. "Abby honey, take a picture of the cake," said one of my aunts, and I did so obediently, and with a few more phones and cameras since suddenly everyone else needed one, too. I helped carry the ham out to the buffet table, then armload after armload of sodas and wine. There was one perk of family gatherings, and that was free food, and good food at that. None of my father's experiments were present; my parents had decided to bring cheese and sausages since it had to travel. I was called in and out as set-up progressed, while Sylvia and Taylor helped with decoration, turning a dusting of white in a grey forest into a warm, candle-lit wonderland. Even the old folding tables looked nice with a proper spread on them, and of course, more candles. I helped my father carry a large vat of mulled wine out, which we set on the woodstove. It smelled amazing, more like cloves and cinnamon than wine, almost cider-like.

"Don't tell your cousins, but I might let you have a sip later, okay?"

"Sure." I smiled and shrugged. It wasn't the first time I got to have a taste, just usually at Easter and Thanksgiving. My mother cast him a look in passing, she'd heard that.

"What? You let me all the—"

"Abby," she said firmly, and that was all she needed to say. It wasn't my battle to fight, and I let her have her stare down with my father as I helped carry out another plate of ham at my aunt's command. I tried to send good thoughts my father's way.

The food was set up, and the decorations were in place, making the whole yard shimmer with candlelight and silver reflecting across the snow, as little flurries blew about, catching the occasional bit of light on their journey. Everyone filed out, Victoria last to follow. She looked almost displeased for a brief moment, a quick cast of judgment crossed her face, and then she lit up with glee. I wondered if anyone else was reading her, but judging by the warm smiles, sentimental looks and cameras flashing, no one else was scrutinizing the moment. That must have been reserved for dealing with moody teenagers and spying. I gave in and stopped thinking so hard, so I could focus on making sure there were some decent pictures of the event.

The ceremony was the same old thing I remembered from mine, and watching Syl's, and Taylor's too. They had all been on this same yard, but Grandmother had overseen them. This one was done by my mother's oldest sister, the new family matriarch with my grandmother away. She did well, or at least she seemed to recall it all, how we escaped the trials, where we came from, and how much our family has grown. There was some family history, and some reminiscing, and of course, lots of baby stories about Victoria. She smiled through them all, fighting the blushing out of her cheeks and trying to be a good sport about it. I could tell she was a bit upset, but no one else did. It ended with her being presented with her ceremonial broom, a beautiful birch and willow with ribbons. That was the only part where I really looked up, having otherwise been eating my way through the candied almonds with Laurie, and sneakily texting Will under the table. I had snapped some photos, for my mom's sake, but the nuts had tempted me from my duties. Most of the other boys didn't seem very interested either. They never got this kind of party, and it was probably a little sparkly for their tastes. It was sparkly for mine, too, especially when a rainbow twinkled and formed above us when she was presented with her broom. She flew up into it, and it exploded in a sea of glitter. Everyone clapped and my aunt and mother were tearing up. I was the out-of-place cynic, shielding my drink from the sparkling barrage of magical girly shrapnel, as I couldn't imagine it tasting any better full of glitter. I didn't really pay much attention to what happened after. I assumed she zoomed around a bit and her mother cried and she got lots of hugs and well-wishes from everyone. I was out of almonds and sneaking more from the tray over. I sent Will a picture of the glitter-coated car, and I could feel the horror in his response.

**{SAVE THE PAINT!]**

Once the buffet was open, resumed my mission of stuffing my face with food while taking a few token pictures. Lady-like behavior went out the window in the presence of a good ham. My father stayed nearby with Laurie, as my mother managed to graze and mingle. Laurie was sulking about the food options. He was pickier than I was, and he only liked things like chicken and mac and cheese, and he was not having anything to do with aunt so-and-so's green bean casserole or some of the traditional dishes from Germany. He gave each tiny portion the same deeply concerned look he had given my father's oatmeal. He finally ate his ham and more almonds. I was a little more used to the traditional dishes of my family, but he'd just been dumped into a far off culinary wasteland, and he wasn't happy for it. My father let him go play eventually, perhaps feeling a little sorry for him. He'd been a good sport, if a miserable one. Dad slipped up on me, nonchalantly passing me a cup. "Go mingle, and don't share that."

I looked down, and smiled just a bit. He did remember. "Thank you." I went off to go bother Sylvia. I felt like I didn't know anyone else. I knew their names and a vague synopsis at best. He uncle something-or-other and was a dental hygienist and had a Labrador. She was a cousin, but we called her aunt, and she liked hummingbirds. That was uncle something was married to aunt someone last year and looked just as scared of me as I was of him. But I didn't really know almost any of them, not enough to connect. I wondered if this is why I was supposed to go mingle, but it looked like everyone else was settling into their own groups now. Last night had been for that, it seemed. I could hear a snowball fight in the making on the opposite side of the house, and I wanted to join in too. I wasn't dressed for it, though, and I knew my mother would go nuts if I got myself snowy and dirty while wearing nice clothes. She was never quite as hard on Laurie for it, I wondered if it was because mine probably cost more. Maybe it was "Boys will be boys," but I was exempt from all that as an almost grown "young woman," as she liked to call me now.

I didn't feel any closer to womanhood than I did on the day I was presented with my broom.

"Wasn't that sweet?" asked Sylvia, grinning with mischief in her eyes. Brynn cooed at me, still bearing a deer-like resemblance as she watched the snow and glitter mix that danced in the air.

"Saccharine, more like."

"Aw, but she just looked so happy and overjoyed."

"That kid has one creepy grin. Like one of those kids in horror movies that walks after you slowly holding a kitchen knife."

"That's harsh. It's more like Veruca Salt, really."

"Daddy, I want another pony." I went wide-eyed and smiled sweetly.

Sylvia recoiled in horror and covered Brynn's eyes. "Don't scare the baby. Or give her ideas." Brynn giggled away and waved her chubby arms.

"Aww, see, she loves it." I turned my slasher grin back on, "Hi Brynn!"

"Okay, correction, stop scaring me," Sylvia squeaked.

"Oh, fine. So, nice party huh?"

"I didn't get a rainbow." I chuckled in a mock pout.

"Oh please, you wouldn't want a rainbow. You'd want it to rain frogs or something."

"Now you see, that would have been a party! They would have been in everyone's hair, the drinks, hopping around, boys catching them, and then poof! Gone." We laughed and speculated, wondering who would cry or scream. Then one statement caught me off guard, when it really shouldn't have.

"You never made a very good girl, Abs."

A million thoughts went through my head, and that weird feeling came over me again. I looked down at my shoes, and shrugged. She was right, I didn't. And I still didn't feel like one, and I certainly didn't feel like the woman I was supposed to magically turn into four years ago on this same yard. I didn't feel a day closer to womanhood, or more in touch with that part of myself. I wasn't even sure that part existed, like one day childhood was suddenly split into future men and women, and not just a bunch of sugared-up monsters running around in circles.

I looked out across the snowy yard at Victoria, as she graciously greeted and interacted with each guest, practically glowing as she made her rounds.  She walked tall, confident and feminine in her traditional dress. It may have been a modern take, but right now she was the iconic little witch girl, who looked like she could turn into a little witch woman, and someday the family matriarch. I remembered wanting to lose my dress and chase squirrels as soon as the ceremony was over. She was everything the family took pride in, and she looked like a real part of it. I wondered if some day she would out grow her snobby way of always looking down her nose, and I wondered what that would make me then. I didn't feel like I'd ever be any closer. I wondered what was wrong with me.

"Abs? Abby? Abbababababigail?" She pulled me from my melodramatic internal monologue with four terrible words.

"Your ham is falling." And the world rushed back in time to save it.

"Schaved." I said after I had stuffed it into my mouth. I looked as triumphant as I could with bulging chipmunk cheeks.

"You gave off a weird aura just then. Never quite felt that one." She arched a brow at me.

"Dunno what it is. It's a thing." I shrugged. "Like…being lost, or having an out of body experience. It's kind of…" I waved my hands around and hoped she would understand. Her expression said she did not. I sighed. "It's weird… It just happens a lot."

"Well, it's not the color of teenage angst. It makes your aura more purple and blue, and gives off a feeling of sorrow and longing and melodrama." She touched her temples and said this in the most psychic way she could manage. "You should take tea of the—"

"You sound like my mom."

"Okay, you should get outside the house and get some more sunlight and maybe go do something active or productive sometime?"

"You still sound like my mom."

"Well, it does help with depression."

"Yeah, so I've heard. I tried that, I just got sore thighs. But hey, I got muscles too." I liked the muscles, but I didn't like the effort of keeping them. All it took was winter to make me squishy again. I was no good at keeping up routine anyway. "It didn't really work, though."

"Vitamin D? Sunshine? Therapy?"

"Never tried the last one. I don't want my parents to think I'm nutty, anyway. It's probably just some kind of phase…" I remembered my cup, and took a sip. It was nice, fruity and spicy. I took only the occasional sip, I knew Dad was counting on me to not do anything stupid. I wasn't going to let him down over half a red plastic cup of "forbidden fruit." I looked up to him too much for that. Not that I would ever admit it.

"It didn't feel normal," she said, but seemed ready to drop the subject. We both knew I was stubborn. There was a long pause, and she looked down at her daughter's smiling face. "We should go inside for a bit, Brynn's getting cold." The baby was looking a little more rosy cheeked than usual, if otherwise completely cheerful. I assumed she must have just simply known. I saw this as an opportunity to get more ham, and maybe some cake. I passed Victoria on the way back. "Good luck, Vick. You have quite the road ahead of you." I smiled and wished I could impart some sort of older and wiser wisdom upon her. No matter how much my mind scrambled, I could not find a single token of feminine wisdom to pass on.

"Thank you Abigail. I look forward to it." She smiled with what I could not place as confidence or sheer smugness, and I had an aching dread that she knew more about this whole growing up thing than I did. I scurried along after Sylvia; my ham suddenly didn't feel as amazing as it had a moment ago. It wasn't going to fix any of my problems. But maybe, cake would. Once inside, I was at the mercy of every aunt, uncle and grown cousin again, an onslaught of "How's school?" "Have you found a college?" "Are you going to study something more in the family?" And a shower of unsolicited and largely useless advice. By the time Brynn was warmed and cake was being cut, I was no closer to solving any of my problems. I felt like dirt, or something even less useful than dirt, like silt or that slime clay makes when it gets too wet. I was no closer to finding out what to do with my life, or what was wrong. My brain as getting foggy, and not with the feeling of being lost or displaced in the way it had before, but with genuine self doubt. I was thankfully blessed with a moment of clarity as my ready-for-the-world little cousin cut into her cake. She smiled for pictures and looked more confident then I would ever be.

For that moment, I accepted the fact that I seemed to basically be failing at life. And that was okay, for now, because at least I still had options. And after a brief wait in line, I also had a piece of cake. It had stars on it.

## Chapter Six

Sylvia and I had exchanged email addresses and phone numbers before parting ways. I had never thought that after three years of relative silence, we'd click back together like the mischievous duo we had been before. She was still the imp behind an innocent façade, the one who never looked like she was up to anything. She said I was still the same old-souled and sarcastic troublemaker that I was before, and I didn't know whether that was a compliment or not. I didn't even know that children could be sarcastic, but my mother agreed on the car ride home. She said Sylvia had pegged me perfectly, and I admit, I spent the next hour half-sulking, half speculating and thinking.

"Where does Sylvia live, anyway?" I realized I had forgotten to ask her.

"She lives with her husband in Pennsylvania."

"Where in Pennsylvania?"

"I'm not sure, just somewhere there."

It wasn't like she had told me Sylvia lived in Rhode Island or Massachusetts. Pennsylvania was long, an agonizing eight hours across on its own. "Call her and ask." My mother sighed, rubbing her neck. It was going to be a long ride back, straight through the night. I alternated texting William and Sylvia through most of the trip, until both had gone to bed, and I was alone. My parents traded driving somewhere in exactly nowhere, a street light flickering softly above, and a gas station sign glowing in the distance. I dozed off reluctantly some time past four AM, and my mother drove on through the night. The world faded in and out, from the darkest until dawn's first light, and all across the state of Pennsylvania.

The world's fastest weed whacker was puttering in the drive when we pulled up some time in the morning. It was in a state called idling, but it sounded like it was fighting for its life. I sleepily emerged from the car and was caught off-guard by Will, who pulled me into a hug so dramatic I hit my cheek on his shoulder. "Abby!" He grinned and shoved me back again, holding my shoulders. I blinked and tried to summon an appropriate response. Too late, he had hugged me again.

"I was gone a weekend," I mumbled.

"But I missed my Isle of Sanity!" I found myself being hugged again, and pulled away in protest. "Abby?"

"I'm going to take a nap. I'll be back out in a while." I mumbled. I shouldered my suitcase, and shuffled inside after my parents. The only awake one among us was Laurie, and my mother was all too happy to let him go over to William's house to play with his little brothers for a while. The house was blanketed in the sweetest quiet, as I found my bedroom, and collapsed on to my old, faithful, too-small bed. I could not recall changing clothes or getting under the blankets, I just collapsed in and let sleep take me.

I didn't fly, not this time. This time I was falling. I watched pieces of the world zoom past me, and I was unable to grab for anything, desperate for something to hold on to. The void was flying at me, as islands of familiarity floated out of reach. I saw my house, disembodied pieces of my street zooming past me on uprooted masses of dirt.

"Aaron, Grab my hand!" screamed a girl. I knew she meant me, for reasons I didn't understand. I didn't stop to thing, I reached down as I was hurtling towards a figure below me, a golden-haired girl in a black dress. My eyes clenched shut as I braced for impact. Our hands met, the sensation of soft, warmth seized me. Someone was clinging to me, as I hung over the edge of the mossy floating island. "Hold on, please hold on, I can explain everything!" I saw the tears in her eyes as she tried to pull me up, but my weight was working against her, and she was going to go over the edge with me. I scrambled for grip. My fingers dug into the dirt as I let go of one of her hands. And then, I slipped. She lunged over the edge, and reached for me. We were briefly so close, and I saw the deepest hazel eyes. And then, we missed each other as she had hurled herself after me in vain. Her sandy hair flew in her face, and she screamed, "Aaron!" And the island flew past me. I'd lost her.

I woke up in a way that only happens in movies. I was upright and panting, with enough force that I had thrown the sheets down to my knees. It was all so vivid, not just whispers and murmurs of surreal landscapes as I was on some fantastic road trip on a penny-powered mechanical horse. It was still vivid and clear in my head, it was the real world I was having trouble grabbing old of right now. I looked in my dresser mirror, and I saw myself, even if something felt different, wrong. I stood with surprising difficulty, and held onto the dresser's edges. It took a long moment to understand who or what I was looking back at. It was the same red-brown hair, and the same brownish greenish eyes, like a murky pond. It was me, but I didn't feel convinced. I wanted the other body back, the one I only recalled as being a flailing mess as I fell, but it was me, and what I saw in the mirror was another creature. I had left myself behind.

And that dark, disconnected feeling, the one that had flirted in and out of my life for years like the monster under my bed… it swallowed me alive.

## Chapter Seven

I had never had a panic attack before. I always assumed it was a lot more like being scared, and a lot less feeling like you were going to die. My heart was in my head my throat, my temples, my hands, like it had shattered itself and was trying to claw its way out. I couldn't think, I could barely breathe, my whole body was shaking and there was nothing I could do to steady it. I thought I was dying. For once, I would have killed for my mother to be spying on me, reading me as she passed my bedroom door. But, she wasn't, and I was alone to find my footing and catch my breath again. I spent a long time on the floor, my cheeks were dapple-printed with carpet fibers when I managed to drag myself into my bed. I was shaking, badly. I closed my eyes and tried to form the strokes and lines of my mental calligraphy. Even my invisible hand was slipping, and I tried to focus on smooth strokes and the shapes of the numbers, but it felt like my ink was going everywhere.

I didn't pull out of it enough to leave my room until I reached two hundred and fifty six. I was still uneasy on my feet; my mind was racing to keep up where it could. I was desperately thirsty but nauseous. I fumbled in the pantry for teabags, watching a box of chamomile and one of mint fall past my face. I let them sit on the floor, and brewed myself an anxious cup of tea. I wanted my mother's guidance to pull itself from the gently steaming cup of tea, the ritual we shared whenever I was upset. But, there was no lit sage in the air, and my mother wasn't at my side. She was only a few rooms away, sleeping, but she was farther away than the alien land of Ohio had been. She was hopelessly out of my reach, and all I was left with was a lonely cup of tea.

I felt humiliated, even if there was no one around to see me. I'd broken down over a stupid dream, and my own damned reflection. I looked down at my hands, and they were not the hands I had seen in my dream. The ones I held out as I fell seemed more real to me, and as I held my cup of tea, I felt trapped in a cage. I was in someone that wasn't quite me. It was a long while before the world started to settle around me, and probably three cups of tea before it made any sense. The feeling which had only shifted in and out of my life had dragged me to places I had never been, and I found myself afraid of my own mind.

I returned to my room for a change of clothes, and then wandered numbly next door to seek out the only other source of familiarity. He was in his garage, door open, and I simply walked in and sat heavily upon the bench, staring at my shoes. I had forgotten to put on my sneakers, still in my boy's dress shoes from the party.

"Nice nap?" he asked, hunched over his project. I must have taken too long to answer, because he was looking at me now, and set down his socket. "You…look like hell," he said. His brows were arched in deep concern, mouth drawn in small, and for once his voice wasn't steeped in sarcasm.

"Yeah. Just tired still, I guess."

"You don't look tired." He paused, looking deep in thought, then added,

"You look like someone ran over your cat then backed up."

"Thank you, William." I sighed and lay on the bench. It was hard aluminum, like they had in gym locker rooms, and my own shoulders were trying to impale me even through my natural padding and hoodie. "I feel more like I'm stuck in something weird and squishy and estrogen-dipped."

"I'm pretty sure that's called being a girl, though I have not first-hand felt the squishy part." He waggled his eyebrows at me and shot me the worst flirtatious grin he could fake without laughing. He dropped it when he realized I wasn't laughing.

"It's weird, Will. Like I'm a body snatching alien who just stole someone else and has no idea what they're doing with it." I stretched out my hand above me and surveyed it carefully. It was mine, the one I always remembered, but it wasn't right. My own body felt like a foreign land I had spent years in. I had mostly gotten accustomed to its quirks, I knew most of the language, and I could almost blend in. But I was still a foreigner, a stranger caught off guard by little hints and pieces and snippets of culture that I would never fully master, and now I direly wished to return home, even if I couldn't recall it. "I am a stranger in a strange land…"

"Your skin is not your own?" I thought for almost a moment that he understood, and then I realized it was just a counter-reference to another old book that no one else our age had read. He smirked and chanted slowly, "Muad-dib, muad-dib."

I sighed and rolled over to glare at him right side up, "I hate you sometimes."

"Hey, me too." Will chuckled.

"Can we go inside for a bit? It's cold."

"You're the one who forgot your coat."

"Oh come on…"

"I'll throw another log on the stove." He stood and shuffled stiff-leggedly, whimpering something about pins and needles as I assumed he was trying to find feeling in his legs again.

"You don't want to go in, maybe play a game? Co-op mode?" I tried my best sad puppy dog eyes. No luck, his back was to me.

"No, everyone's home, and it's kind of loud in there. I mean, there's Trickster and Badger playing with Truck, which is a recipe for a ruckus, and I think Max's in there." The real reason came out, his older brother was home. They shared a room, but he was very rarely in it.

"Does a widdle noise hurt the bunny's ears?" I teased. I was finally feeling better, since I had been pulled wildly off-topic from my previous thoughts. I had my best friend back, in all of his ill-tempered grumpy glory at the moment.

"Not cool, not a bunny." He tossed a log into the stove with a crackle of spark and flame.

"But you're the cutest little fuzzy—"

"Jerk." He sat down with his machine again, looking surly and focused, which wasn't a bad look on him now that I stopped and examined it. It made him look almost serious, like he wasn't the guy who practiced his Ministry of Silly Walks routine.

I didn't speak up for a long while, but had no fear that he was actually mad at me. He had gone from annoyed to focused, and had probably forgotten about everything. "Want to go play co-op at my house?" I asked, then added "My parents are asleep…" I spoke in my best "late-night hotline" voice and tried to imitate his eyebrow wiggle. He snorted and laughed.

"Okay, you've sold me. I'll get the disk, you go wake up the Xbox and quell its angry spirits with some lavender, or a human sacrifice, or you know, whatever you witches use to ward off the red ring of death." This would have been offensive from almost anyone else, but I always found Will's irreverence refreshing. He might not be from a witch family, but he was on the other side, like me.

## Chapter Eight

I felt like the dream had unlocked something in me. Somewhere in my mind, what had always been a hairline crack had become a steady trickle. The feeling was in no way new, the cracks had been there for as long as I could remember with the occasional drips slipping through. Sometimes I'd worry what was on the other side, as little pieces of it came into my life against my consent. Now it never stopped, it was a constant, nagging presence that was there from when I woke to when I collapsed into bed. I thought I was losing my mind, and I wondered why I couldn't just deal with it, like I had for most of the life I could remember. But no matter where I turned, I was still in the cage, and I felt like the rest of the world was starting to pass me by.

Spring had slipped up on me before I knew it. It was Connecticut spring, not real spring like they showed on Easter cards and television. Connecticut spring meant that you could still have snow in the beginning of May, just like Connecticut fall meant that you could have foot-high blizzards in October. The calendar said spring. Technically, the calendar said April 15. The grass was just starting to wake up, and the trees were little dots of color on gray husks, and this morning, it was all dusted in another coat of snow.

The world's fastest weed whacker didn't start this morning, but I could hear the familiar clunking of William's toolbox as it migrated across the driveway. I wondered whose car he was working on. Usually, I would stay in bed until I heard my father get up, but this time I threw on whatever clothes I could find and went to bother Will. He was leaning over his brother's car, a used convertible Mustang that William had practically rebuilt for him in exchange for the occasional ride to school or Vespa part off the internet.

"Do you ever sleep like a normal person?" I checked my phone in my pocket, it was 6:15 and just minutes past sunrise.

"Why should I? Stop and listen."

I waited for him to say something and gave him a confused look.

"No siblings. No parents. No barking husky across the street." He was right; the world was dead silent aside from his fidgeting. He grinned at me, like he had found the answer to something he'd been searching for his whole life, and then I realized, he had.

William hated being inside, he hated being crammed into a small house with six siblings. He hated sharing his room with his brother. In waking up early, he'd found a way around it all, and I hadn't realized it until now, after putting up with three years of his rattling around at sunrise.

"Besides, we hares are crepuscular creatures," he said, like it was something noble. For all I knew at the moment, it might have been, but he was never one to miss a dumb look being thrown his way. He looked amused, almost smug "Well, somebody sleeps in Bio. It means we're most active at dusk and dawn."

"By that reasoning, you should be the one sleeping through class."

"And ruin a 4.0? How else am I going to get into medical school?"

I realized even he had planned this out more than I had. I thought we were on the same page, with over a year left to go, what was there to worry about right now, in April? I thought maybe there was someone else in this world who was just as unsure about where they were going, but at least was planning to go somewhere.

"I thought you were going to be a mechanic." I had no bench to sit on and leaned on the car. He'd never said it, aside from maybe a second grade report on "what I want to be when I grow up." Then I recalled he picked lion tamer back then anyway. It seemed obvious to me, like it was an already set in stone fact. He was always under something, oil smudged, wrist-deep in some machine's entrails. He was happy that way, and I couldn't understand why he would want to go do something that wasn't what he did every single day for fun. Until that moment, I had envied Will, because it seemed like where he was going in life was going to let him do what he loved and not starve to death.

"Medical school?" I stumbled over those words; he'd not answered me in the first place.

"I want to go help others, I want to save lives. My grades are fantastic, and I love all the squishy science stuff. My dad told me about what medical care was like when he visited reservations, maybe I can actually go do some good for my own people. And I don't mean just Natives, I mean, us Weres can already be thrown out of hospitals if we don't document everything like we're smuggling in guns in our boots. And so can you witches. And we're already almost always some racially ambiguous scary thing to most of suburbia…" He trailed off on his rant. I could tell he was getting genuinely upset. He had stopped tightening the belt he was working with and was actually looking at me with the same fierce passion I usually only saw devoted to an ailing engine.

"So you want to be a doctor?"

"I want to be a doctor where people can't afford one, Abby. I don't know, maybe something like Doctors Without Borders, or go west to the reservations, I mean, we have a twenty five percent chance of being born Were, and everyone's still terrified of that. But I'm not. I don't care if you're a were or a witch or fae or elf or who knows what else is out there in the world that gets branded and labeled and treated like a walking weapon."

Something had gotten into him today, and I couldn't tell just what by looking at him. And then, it hit.

"You got your license, didn't you?" I asked. It had slipped my mind, I was so used to him going everywhere on the weed whacker, I had forgotten he was taking driving lessons too. He didn't even tell me he'd taken the test, let alone passed it. His expression hardened in a way that wasn't just being a surly rabbit. He dug into his pocket, and pulled the card from his wallet. Right under his height and across from the little pink organ donor heart, were two little letters after the label "Misc." W.C.

"Were-Creature," I said, looking at it in disbelief.

"They got progressive in the last five years, now it doesn't say "Were Wolf." It's so if I get pulled over, they know to wait and see if I'll turn into a cougar and chew someone's leg off."

"But you're a bunny."

"Yeah, exactly. If I turned because I was freaked out, you know what would happen? I'd hop around like an idiot, hide under a seat and probably just crap all over things. But now a cop, or airport security, or, anybody knows that if they meet me they might have to reach for the really big gun just in case I turn into a fucking grizzly bear!" His voice echoed down the street, neither of us had realized he was yelling until the silence struck us after he had stopped.

"Shit," he almost whispered. "I hope I didn't just fucking out us." He whimpered, mumbling a string of terrified profanity, his arms were shaking as he braced himself on the front bumper. Tears were welling up in his eyes, he was sure he had blown our cover, and until that moment, I had forgotten we were hiding.

We spent the next half hour almost silent, as we waited for the cops to show up for a noise disturbance, with their extra big guns for the were-bunny and the undocumented witch. We were sure some busy-body neighbor was going to ruin our lives, but nothing happened, no one came. We were saved by one guy's unusual sleeping habits, and the world had slept though our outbursts. It started to set in that I was in danger too, if anything happened. I was so much at the ready to protect Will, that I had forgotten that I was an almost grown witch without any identification. I was almost illegal just for being nearly 18 and alive. I didn't have my license yet, and I wasn't sure if I wanted to drive now. I didn't want to buy a bottle of wine and have the clerk see the "W.I." for witch. Even then, I knew I would need a state ID card, a passport, some piece of paper to reveal my status for the safety of everyone else around me. I sometimes forgot how secretive our families still had to be, and how we had found an oasis in each other, as magical castaways. I had forgotten about the long talks and coffee our parents shared after I had found William in the yard. All I knew at the time was that I had found a bunny who was also a boy, who I liked better as a bunny. What they must have found was a little shred of safety in our fake-normal suburban lives. They had to stay silent and normal, when they were probably just so desperate to find someone else they could talk to about this.

It was an almost silent, painfully quiet sort of morning, as we waited for the rest of the world to wake up, just to show it wasn't afraid of us. My mind was racing with ideas of the whole of the neighborhood hiding away in their homes, locking their doors and guarding their children from two harmless teenagers just trying to change out an alternator. William crossed by me and climbed in the car. He turned the key, and the engine came alive, but he didn't come back out. I leaned to look around the car's hood, and saw him with his forehead resting on the steering wheel. I did all I knew how to do, I just waited, watching the fine dusting of snow sneak off into the grass and hide in the crevices and shade. He eventually got out, after killing the engine. "Had to reset the internal computer." And I pretended that I didn't know that was a lie.

"I have to get ready," I trailed off, then added, "Can you give me a ride?"

"Yeah, sure. I'll get the Vespa going, or I'll tell Brian he has to. He owes me." He shut the hood and headed inside to a house that was just waking up. I returned to mine, and startled my father by slipping through the garage door into the kitchen.

"You're up early." The first syllable was especially loud, as he'd nearly thrown the spatula he was holding. I might have startled him, not that he'd admit it.

"Yeah. Decided to go help William with a car."

"Oh, well, that's nice."

I wanted to tell him about the morning, how we might have just shouted out everything to the world around us. I wanted to be reassured, and I was terrified about what might happen if even one busybody had heard us and wanted to make everything their business. What if we needed to move or Will had to? Everything was in a tenuous state of balance and whole world was getting ready to fall in around me.

I wasn't very interested in my breakfast, and I had another cup of tea, because it reminded me of calming back down with lit sage and my mother at my side. She was in the far off world of in bed, and I wasn't going to wake her. She would wonder why I was upset, and then I would have to tell her.

"You okay, Pumpkin?" my dad asked.

"Yeah, just still tired." I lied, and gave a strip of bacon a nibble of acknowledgement. Laurie was lurking next to me, looking remarkably like a shark as he eyed my mostly uneaten plate. He never got to steal it, as William had stopped by, like he did every morning. "Bacon?" I offered.

"Best thing I have heard all morning." His voice was drained with a sort of forced cheer. He was hiding an emotional limp, trying to blend in again. I surrendered the bacon, and then the toast was taken captive, and my little shark brother had no interest in a solitary, defenseless poached egg.

I excused myself to get things for school, remembering at the last moment that my slippers were not actually my shoes, and threw together my backpack. I greeted Will, laden down with half a library over my shoulder. At least today, we didn't have to take the bus. We would ride in style in a convertible sardine can with one of the most popular boys in school.

# Chapter Nine

It was always a little awkward sitting next to Brian, riding up front with a boy I was told was very attractive. Not by himself, or thankfully Will, but it was a common bit of bathroom chatter I would overhear every now and then, or locker side gossip about who he was or wasn't dating. I didn't see much in him. I liked boys but not ones quite like him. Brian had a squared jaw and prominent eyebrows, and a near-constant confident sort of smirk that I had known as his default expression for as long as he had lived next door. He'd taken after his father's side, and he looked almost as much like his Navajo half as William looked like a displaced beaky English boy with a tan. He was athletic, in the basketball or track and field kind of way, and he was one of the "popular boys." I didn't think of him as that when he was the nice guy next door who shared a bedroom with my best friend and always got Laurie's toys off the roof.

I didn't hate him for it. I wasn't sure if many people who knew Brian could actually hate him. He wasn't the dumb high school sitcom jock who threw kids in dumpsters, not a raging testosterone-dripping jerk who left a wake of broken hearts and wounded nerds in his path. He was always friendly, helpful, and fairly bright. Not medical school 4.0 bright like William, who was almost hugging his knees in the back seat of the car and desperately just trying to make himself fit. He was, to steal a college-prep term I heard every single day, well-rounded. He was a great athlete, had good grades, was approachable, and even did a little community service with their mother. The only trait I truly envied in him was that he could be out about what he was and still find friends.

It was a freak accident, the day he shifted at school. William told me it was just the wrong time of the seasons, hormonal problems and a little too much exertion that set things in motion. He was always very quick to remind me that spontaneous shifting wasn't normal. When Brian went for the 400 meter dash, something he couldn't control kicked in. I knew girls who still gleefully talked and giggled about how his clothing "exploded" and a young elk had gone galloping at full speed across the track. William told me the other side of the story, about going combing through the woods with his parents and police with search dogs being on the scene. I knew the side that no one else at school did, as over three exhausting days, the world came to a screeching halt for his family. I knew the side that was their mother sobbing and driving circles between exits on Interstate 84 hoping and praying that she wouldn't see an elk leap out into traffic, come tumbling down a cliff, or just simply her son dead on the side of the road. I remembered William almost living at our house for a week, as his parents considered moving, home schooling, or sending Brian off out west to go stay with family who could handle his "condition."

Brian had gotten lucky, it was the kind of lucky that was like surviving a lightning strike. He showed up safe and sound, completely calm, and buck naked at a local taco stand. Rumor has it he just walked in, and up to the counter, and asked for a number 8 crunchy and to use their phone. He wasn't hurt, and he narrowly avoided indecent exposure charges. The incident had nearly made him a hero at school between the sheer nonchalant awesomeness of his return, and the fact that he had evidently terrified the other teams into losing in almost everything when the competition finally resumed. William tended to whine that it was cool for him because he was a cool animal. I had to admit that may have had just a little to deal with it, but I also thought that Brain could have turned into a fox, a coyote, or even a raven and still walked back just looking cool and "exotic." I thought he made it through for the better because he was already just a likeable guy who let things roll off his back.

William said he would have been socially executed had he turned into a rabbit like him.

I didn't feel the excitement of showing up in the same car as him that some girls I knew said I should have. It just felt like a ride, a little less cold and wet than the weed whacker. I was just riding along with the neighbor boy, and not the smoldering beast I was told Brian was supposed to be. It was hard to think smoldering beast when I was being serenaded by rowdy Irish-American punk music blasting from every speaker in the car. It was one of Will's CDs. Music seemed to be the only thing we all had in common, aside from a genetic condition known as "magic," but honestly, that came up a lot less than Flogging Molly.

# Chapter Ten

I changed in the back of the locker room for gym, doing my best to square myself into the corner and vanish. I took on the task of changing with the most utility that I could, I didn't brush my hair back into something clean and stylish, I didn't make sure my gym clothes looked nice once they were on me. I wanted to vanish, and my middle and elementary school days of changing in a bathroom stall were no longer options. There was nothing about the act that I wanted to prolong. In, clothes off, clothes on, leave. On the return trip, I'd add a quick shower to the routine if I could find a secluded spot to slide into, or I would just mill around in the back of the locker room, get my hair wet in the sink, and make a break for it before anyone realized I had skipped the shower.

"Aren't you a little big to be wearing those?" someone behind me asked, and the tone in which she said 'those' was like someone had stuck a slug under her nose.

I looked down in mild confusion, "Shorts?" I was a bit on the squishy side, but no one had told me shorts had a weight limit, especially when they were required for gym. I knew that voice, and she was the closest thing I had ever known to a true high school drama mean girl. She wasn't quite as popular and tended to be a thorn in the side of even some of the "cool" people.

"I have never—" There was that tone again, "Seen you wear a normal bra. You know, something cute."

"It's gym; you wear sports bras in that, unless you want an under-wire mishap to stab you to death."

"I don't think you even own an underwire."

I turned and looked at her, trying to hold my cool, and just looked down at her "cute" pink push-up.

"Yeah, I'm pretty sure I don't need to." I never took pride in my chest, in fact, I was usually trying to flatten it away, but I knew that one hit a mark. Jenny had been whining about her cup size since before little girls even need bras. I looked down at her and tried my best judgmental eyebrow quirk. I was more annoyed than anything by her; this wasn't the kind of bullying that made me feel like an after-school special and start sobbing on the floor. It was the kind that made me want to vigorously beat the inner bitch out of her with a Literary History textbook.

"Whatever you say, Miss training bra and cargo pants. Ugh, you dress like my brother." She sneered and strutted off with her nose in the air and a perfect catwalk gait that I felt was wasted on someone with no chest and a permanent scowl.

"You should have asked her if that meant her brother wears a bra and cargo pants." Will and I sat back on the bleachers and talked, while we traded out who was on the gym floor. In his shorts and loose T-shirt, he was all knees, elbows, and shoulder blades even more so than usual.

"Ah! You're right! Why does that always have to happen?"

"The best comebacks always hit you later, I should know, I have siblings, ones that fight back."

"Rough. Laurie just yells at his age." I was still having trouble shaking the feeling I'd gotten in the locker room. I hadn't been too terribly bothered by Jenny's harassment in general; I was used to it and didn't honestly find her bright enough to feel too harassed by it. She was just lashing out, as Will would remind me back when she did bother me. Now she was just an annoyance, a hundred and ten pound mosquito with a catty streak.

I was more upset by when she had approached me, not her method of attack. The locker room never did sit right with me, and not just because everyone was naked. No matter how old I got, it was still an alien land filled with scenes and rituals I didn't understand, no matter how much older I got. I always just assumed I would grow into this "girl" thing, my mother said it was perfectly normal, but at almost seventeen and a year and some change left of school, I had my doubts. I was still just as lost and terrible at this whole girl thing. I sat back and watched the skirmish, thankful that I wasn't in right now. I preferred more one-on-one activity to the usual team tasks, call me antisocial I guess. I liked it when we weren't divided on the floor by sex either. William and I kicked ass at ping-pong doubles tournaments, and I was brutal with a foil in my hands the few times we did fencing. It wasn't often Mrs. Bridges pulled that equipment out of storage, it was easier to pass off some balls and keep most of the room amused. I watched the girls' side and the boys' side, at different ends of the court, playing their own games. Mrs. B. blew the whistle and called William's name along with a handful of other boys, and a few girls that were thankfully not me. I'd dodged another round, and would probably be playing after this one. "Go on, bunny-boy." I chuckled. He gave me the "I hate you" look and slouched his way down the stairs. He could do wonders with a car, but his hand-eye coordination was hilarious at best when he didn't have some object in his hand as the mediator. I watched him careen through the game with great enthusiasm and very little skill. I wondered if somewhere under there, he wanted to be the star athlete like his brother, but nature wasn't quite on his side as he blundered through every move, just a step and a half behind everyone else. I watched them start what would be an inevitable loss, not even a close match as five scrawny guys were up against two track stars and a boy who would be a bull moose if he were a were-creature. Or maybe a Kodiak bear. William got the ball, just in time for the moose to trip and stagger sideways into him. They both went down with a fleshy smack, and the ball bounced off towards freedom as Mrs. B. went to check on the situation. Will pulled himself out from under the moose, who looked to mumble an apology and go after the ball. My friend climbed shakily to his feet, unsteady as he walked a weak circle in a haze.

"Chad, you're in. Will, catch your breath." Mrs. Bridges barked.

William nodded numbly and headed in my general direction. He returned to his spot, slinking along, still red-faced and sweaty. I moved over. "Well that was… entertaining," I remarked. He shot me a glare from behind his sweat-clumped hair, and leaned on his knees to catch his breath. It was an oddly severe reaction for being minorly squashed, and I wondered if something more severe had happened, maybe he'd hit his head, or that tank had crushed a rib."Will?" I hesitated and touched his arm. His skin prickled and shuddered under my touch, and I watched his pupils pin in. He started to stand and dropped.

His body fell limply down two levels, and when he hit for sure, he was suddenly no longer my best friend. Something brown and fluffy made a break for it.

## Chapter Eleven

Chaos had broken out, and the gym was suddenly in a panic over one little rabbit. Girls flung themselves out of his way, and clumsy boys flung themselves at him. "Stop you'll hurt him!" I yelled and plowed my shoulder full-force into a guy who was mid-tackle. He lost balance and skidded out. He cursed and scrambled to shove back. Someone else dove after him, landing square on the fleeing rabbit and trying to grapple with Will as he slipped away. My best friend squirmed free and bolted at full pelt for shelter. He was running for his life. His mind wasn't in there anymore.

Mrs. B. was blowing her whistle and shouting for everyone to leave the gym right this moment and regroup in the halls. I ignored her as I rammed the rabbit chaser in the side, "Leave him alone!" My shoulders and chest were pounding as I took a blow right to the collar as he pushed back at me. I whirled and tried to catch a glimpse of my loose friend and took a sudden hit to the sternum with a well-aimed fist. I saw stars and wheezed, staggering back into the bleachers. I'm sure he shouted something at me, they always shout when they hit, but the world abruptly became silent, and I watched the light crackle and twist in the air. Timed slowed for a moment. I stared down the guy, the one who'd tackled my friend. I locked eyes, and my rage came to a boil. I didn't think, no chanting, no ritual, it all just came naturally. I held out my hands, and felt the space in front of me explode.

My attacker suddenly and violently flew back, as every feeling I could summon pulled itself together and released in his direction. He was no longer full of anger and looking for a fight but wide-eyed and practically pissing himself in fear when I managed to get to my feet. I hadn't laid a finger on him, but there was no question that last blow was all my doing, even if I didn't know how it had happened. He bolted, terrified. The room was cleared, except for me as Mrs. Bridges slammed shut the doors. I knew why, at least logically, she needed to handle the majority and get the situation under control out there first, and there was no way to do so with Will and I both on the loose. We had been so terrified this morning, of being found out or having our cover blown, and now it was all over. I shuffled aimlessly for what felt like hours, looking around trash cans and under bleachers for my friend. My head was full of fog, and my ears were ringing, "Will?" I called, voice warbling. Nothing. He was lost now, long gone now in the wake of what I'd done. There was no rabbit to be found under the bleachers or skirting the edges of the room.

I heard screams and giggles erupt in an adjacent hall, and rushed to see my best friend flung by a single, well-aimed kick. He was a rag doll in flight, and only came to life again when his feet hit the ground. He ran off in a mad scramble. "Do not touch him!"I snarled at Will's aggressor. The air crackled again, a locker buckled, students ran. I couldn't stop and think on the situation, my best friend was running for his life.

I didn't wait for Mrs. Bridges to come to our rescue, just I went chasing after him at full speed. "Please come back!" I didn't realize I had been crying until I heard my own choked voice, stumbling over a sob. He didn't slow down, not even for me. I was just another big, horrifying thing that was after him. I lunged and put no effort in cushioning my fall, as I braced my elbows to not crush my best friend.

In any of the books I read, right now would be when he'd turn back into my best friend, and thank me for his rescue. Right then would be when he would miraculously turn back into a boy, safe in the arms of his friend. For a moment, that is what I was sure was going to happen. I didn't expect for him to make the most horrifying scream once I seized him. I also didn't expect those cute, big rabbit feet to come crashing into my jaw with claws scrambling. He fought with every ounce of strength in him, clawing and kicking at my face and arms as he wailed like a sobbing infant. I had never heard a rabbit scream before. I had also never felt a rabbit fight before; he was not the garden ball of fluff I had caught when I was six, and I realized I was grappling with a full-grown desert hare.

I clung and shifted, and managed to wedge his legs under his body and away from my face. He bucked under my arms, trying to hop free of my grasp. "Don't worry Abby, I've got a cage." Mrs. Bridges had come to my rescue, and I was so thankful that she didn't sound scolding of either of us, at least for the moment. My stomach twisted in a knot as she took him by the scruff of the neck and pulled him out of my arms. I noticed the pink smearing his fur, and her horrified expression, before I noticed my own bloodied arms. I hesitantly touched my jaw and didn't want to look at my hand.

"I know I'm fuc-… I'm in a lot of trouble, but can I go clean up?" I was struggling to hold it together as I watched Will throw himself into the sides of the cage, his eyes wide and his sides heaving. He was still terrified, even though he'd been rescued. He'd gotten out of all of this unharmed, and he was still waiting for one of use to kill him. I was never good at the sight of blood, and my knees nearly buckled as I saw that I was leaving drips of it all over the hallway after standing. Mrs. B. bit her lip, and nodded. "Use the one by my office; I'll get the first aid kit." She followed me with the caged hare, still thrashing and flinging himself around in his little wire box. I dragged myself into the restroom and finally looked in the mirror. My chin and neck were scribbled with red, and I didn't want to look at my arms. I turned on the water, and rinsed them before I could even look down. I found myself repeating the same mantra of "Oh fuck" over and over as I tried to wash up and stem the flow with the brown sandpaper towels in the dispenser. All I was succeeding in doing was bleeding on everything.

The last thing I expected was my towel-clad best friend to be the next person through the bathroom door. He didn't look to be expecting me, either. We stared at each other a long moment, both of us pale and ragged, before he finally said something.

"You're in the men's room."

"Well fuck you." I glared and kept mopping at my arm. His next words were even less romantic.

"Okay… I'm going to go throw up now." And he scrambled for a stall and did. I gave up in my efforts to clean myself up and went back to Mrs. B's office with brown paper towels plastered to my neck and arms.

"He just changed back, he didn't look injured," said Mrs. Bridges, setting the cage on the swivel wing-back chair behind her desk.

"Yeah, he's just sick now." I was running out of energy to care about my current state, my heart was still pounding but my adrenal system was giving up on trying to care about any of this.

"Is that normal?" She grabbed a first-aid kit the size of a brief case and started to patch me up.

"Yeah, especially when its stress induced…" I stood rigidly as she gauzed and taped my arms, and started applying butterfly bandages to my chin.

"Is there a risk he'll just turn back again?"

"No… he's too tired."

"You know a lot about his condition." At least now I knew she was sympathetic towards what we were, no one called it a condition if they wanted us removed from society. They called it a power if they saw it as a threat, like we were super-villains, and not just winners of the genetic freak lottery.

"I guess so." I held back the urge to tell her that she should too, if she was his teacher, someone who would deal with him every day. She would have known if a student was epileptic or fatally allergic to bees, and how to handle the situation, but she seemed to be barely aware of the chance he might spontaneously turn into a rabbit. She had no idea how to handle what had happened, and I was getting angrier by the moment. I struggled to regain my focus, letting my mind paint "1, 2, 3..." in imaginary calligraphy, and the world started to slow down. I didn't realize until then that that magical "crackle" was hovering in the air again. I took another breath, and tried to put aside my judgment again. It was going to get me into serious trouble, and for all I knew, maybe his were status was protected by the same law that didn't require you to disclose your medical history. Even still, I was upset. She should have had a better control of the situation, and not just let it all go to hell. I even blamed her for whatever it was I did, and I still wasn't sure what that was.

"Did he change back or…?"

"I used the injection like his record says." Well, that explained why he was stuck in the bathroom with a shifting hangover. That didn't usually happen naturally, it was a side-effect of the medication. I had stuck around through many a crash when it happened in our house, or his if his parents couldn't mind him. I had even changed him back myself, once. I hated doing it, and watching it, I liked letting him live it out and become himself again.

I didn't see William again until we were sitting outside the principal's office, dressed and patched up, and avoiding each other's gaze entirely. I glanced to my side at him, and he was looking ready to cry, biting his lip and constantly shifting his hand, finally settling to chew on his knuckle. His brow was furrowed, and eyes pink and glossy. What little social life he had, we both had, was about to go up in smoke. He looked like he knew his life was over. For all I knew, it might be.

## Chapter Twelve

We met with the principal and our parents separately. First Mr. Kenmore heard from Mrs. Bridges, and the student I had "assaulted." They were throwing that word around a lot, like I had just up and punched him in the face. Actually, they said it like I had snapped and thrown him across the room. Mrs. Bridges was at least neutral, she could not help but talk in her "coach" voice, and wasn't hard to overhear. She was fair, and even sympathetic, but she didn't hold anything back when describing how I had tackled several students, and what she described as being a "telekinetic incident. No matter how neutral her language was, it sounded I was the bully who had used excessive force in a very minor situation, but at least she spared William as an innocent party.

It was probably for the best that she did. He was holding together less and less as the interrogation wore on, and when he was called in, I could not even hear his voice. He emerged, pale and shaking as his parents arrived. His mother's eyes were practically alight, she was ready to take someone down, and at the moment, that looked like her son. He cowered and let out a very audible squeak. Conversations started quietly, as the three of them went back into the office.

I could only catch snippets here and there through the door as he talked with William, once more making him retell the entire situation in detail. Mostly all I heard was his mother raising her voice and the occasional attempt at commanding tone from the guy in charge. I could tell he was being cowed by Will's mother, and I almost couldn't blame him. If she could shift, she'd be a grizzly bear. Maybe he didn't know she couldn't. I heard a lot of the same words being thrown around from religion to disability to medical condition, even a brief insinuation that William chose to shift, which threw his mother into another bear moment. Something fell on the floor as she very clearly bellowed, "How dare you?" The secretary cowered, and so did I. Things became much more restrained after William explained things, and his mother started to bring up anti-bullying groups, and mentioned lawyers.

Suddenly it was much less of a choice and much more of a disability. William asked to be excused a moment, and he passed through the waiting room in a hurry, probably still feeling the kick of the shot. When he was gone, things got interesting and loud. She wasn't holding back any more, as the school was now inches away from legal action on a discrimination case, as well as rampant neglect for handling a medical situation.

"Mrs. Lagai, he could have severely harmed a student!" protested the windbag.

"Mr. Kenmore, my son is a rabbit. He runs as much a risk of harming anyone as a loose squirrel. As far as I am concerned, you allowed my son to be injured repeatedly, chased, and bullied while in the middle of severe medical distress. I advise you make your next choices very carefully."

And it was by the power of a potential mother bear that William avoided suspension, though it was gently suggested he take a few days off to recover. His father had stayed largely quiet through this, though not fearfully so.

"Of course, we will be needing further medical documentation to properly excuse him—" And it started up again. My own mother arrived while the second wind of fighting was going strong. She had tied her hair back in a loose braid with strands of hair escaping here and there and wore no make-up. Her black-framed glasses sat on her nose, and I knew I was likely in a lot of trouble if she had come in such a hurry that she hadn't even put in her contacts or gone with the more fashionable frames. There were the emergency glasses, which meant that the call had woken her in the middle of the "night." I was at the mercy of my principal and a third-shift worker. She smiled politely, but her gaze was intense, and when our eyes met, I knew I was screwed.

"Mom, I—"

"Not a word, not now. Explain everything in there, to both of us." She lowered her voice, "And don't you do that, young lady," she said when I was going to test the waters and try to see what was really on her mind, and even though she couldn't feel if I was, I decided this might be a good time to listen to that command, for once. I dearly wished Dad would have been to come; he was always much gentler and never quite as severe. Unlike Will, I didn't have a grizzly bear on my side, I was about to be locked in a room with one.

William slipped in and lingered in the doorway, as things wound down. And by winding, down it seemed to be an agreement that lawyers were going to be called, and no further conversation was going to happen. His mother exited the doorway with an almost dramatic flourish of the door, walking with purpose. She did not look like the same small, plump English housewife I said hello to almost every day. William flattened himself against the wall and went pale, and her expression softened immediately. It was no longer determination fringed with rage, and she once more looked soft and motherly again.

"Will, dear, we're going to go home," said his mom, in a starkly soothing tone for someone who had moments before been out for blood. She met eyes with my mother, and touched her arm, before cupping her hands. Her expression was warm and hopeful, even if her cheeks were still flushed from shouting. "Ellie, It's not the kids' fault. We know a great lawyer; don't say anything you don't need to."

My mom went from tense and almost defensive, to confused, and I saw her arch and twist her brow into a very inquisitive stare, and I knew she was reading Mrs. Lagai. Her posture relaxed slowly, and she nodded, slowly and knowingly. "Thanks Grace…" Mom turned her gaze back at me, and I tried not to look smug, but she obviously knew what was exactly on my mind.

"I tol—"

"Zip it, Abigail." She did not like being wrong, but at least I had an ally now. We entered Mr. Kenmore's office next, and I could tell quickly that he had even less of an idea on how to manage my mother. She sat down, and listened quietly and intently as I told the entire story. When it came to my "assault" as he kept calling it, he started to be the aggressor.

"So what exactly did you do? You put a spell on him or something?"

My mother tensed at his generalization, but outwardly only seemed to shift slightly in her chair, leaning forward and looking over her glasses.

"I don't know what happened sir. I genuinely don't. I was angry; he was going to hurt my friend." I bit my lip, and squared my shoulders as I looked down at the balding man behind his barricade of a desk, "He could have killed him."

"I think that's a bit dramatic, Abigail. Your use of force was absolutely excessive. You could have killed him or anyone in that room."

"Not as easily as they would have killed Will." I realized instantly that that probably wasn't the best thing to say. I had just admitted I could kill someone, and I didn't even know how I attacked or how to control it.

"You should be expelled; we have a zero tolerance policy on violence in this—"

"You tolerated it against William!"

"I assure you that student will be dealt with immediately."

"When why isn't he in here right now defending himself?"

"Abigail I think you—" He started to rise from his desk, and slid back into his seat as my mother's voice brought a sudden chill to the room, and we both looked back at her command.

"Abby, I will handle this. Mr. Kenmore, why isn't the student who accosted and pursued William not being dealt with first?"

"I didn't, well, I don't think."

"You don't think he's as much of a threat, is that correct?" She rose from her chair almost commandingly. Her posture and tone would not allow any attention to be pulled away.

"Well, he didn't assault a-"

"Mr. Kenmore, he did assault a student, a student who was being afflicted with health issues at the time. He tackled and could have very easily crushed him." She stared down her nose at him, and spoke slowly and gently, like she was addressing a small child that was having trouble understanding things. Her tone had gone frigid.

"I'm sure it was accidental."

"Abby, was it?"

"No, when Moose-, er, when Barry fell on him before he changed, that was an accident. Greg, however, chased him down and tried to jump him."

"Mr. Kenmore, that doesn't sound accidental to me, does it sound so to you?"

"Well, it's a natural reaction to a loose animal—" And he knew he had made a very big mistake. My mother approached his desk and stared down. "My neighbor's son is not an animal. He is a very bright boy with a very promising future, and you are being very, very hurtful to call him that." She rested her hand on the top of his desk and leaned over towards him.

He tried to regain composure, "Ma'am, I cannot just allow Abigail to walk away from this without punishment. There are dire repercussions to fighting, and she damaged school property."

My mother looked back accusingly and I shrunk, “A locker, someone had just kicked Will.”

Her focus snapped back to him with a predatory intensity. “And why is that student not in here. Are his parents on the way? I didn’t see anyone else in the waiting area.”

“Well, he has yet to be identified…” He started to trail off.

“Abby, please go get your things and wait in the car, I’ll be out very shortly.” Her face cracked into an intense smile, and I saw a bit of cousin Victoria in her cold and calculating eyes. I admit, I was happy to flee the scene and waited to see a solid oak desk and balding principal go through the picture window on the other side of that office.

Unfortunately, I didn’t get such a show, just my mother emerging from the school standing very tall, expression still thinly veiled ferocity. In her black sweater and slacks, she did not remind me of a witch, or even my own mother, right now I felt that the care was being approached by a barely tame black panther. She sat, and straightened her hair, and let out a short yet volumous sigh.

“You’re suspended.”

# Chapter Thirteen

"Shit." I cringed and waited for the tongue-lashing to follow.

"Yeah, you got that right." My mother leaned forward and rubbed her temples.

"That's insane, I mean, how the… For how long?"

"Two weeks."

"F—" Survival instinct kicked in, and I realized I didn't want to risk it twice, "Will I even pass this year?"

"You might have to make it up over the summer, but I won't let them fail you. I think I need to talk to a lawyer." She turned on the car and backed out of her parking spot. The world was grey, and we were at that one magical time of day when the streets were actually somewhat clear for a change.

"Did he say anything else?"

"He… recommended a few psychologists. It's the only sense he made."

"Mom I'm not crazy."

"I don't think you are, Abby." I wasn't sure if she meant that she didn't find me crazy or was worried I was. The car crept up over the speed limit, she always speeded when she was stressed. "But it might be good for you to talk to someone, especially if things are manifesting themselves so violently."

I leaned on the car door, trying to pull my thoughts together. "It was just a one-time thing, it's not like I've been quietly brooding away planning to magically obliterate everyone who crosses me."

"But you have been upset about something." I shrunk in my seat and realized she knew. What was almost less heartening was that she didn't know what it was either, this feeling that had been following me around for as long as I could recall. She sighed, and I knew I had just been read. I watched dull residential streets go by, "Just like you are right now."

"You don't have to keep doing that." I sighed and tried to scrunch myself up, as though it would somehow be better protection from her getting inside my head.

"I worry about you, Abby. I never would have expected to have to come in and get you like this, or hear you attacked a student like—"

I whipped in place to look at her, "He started it!" I couldn't believe she was taking his side in all of this. I thought she was my ally.

"And you don't have to finish it." Her voice went cold. "You could have really hurt someone like that, and you have almost no training on how to handle your abilities."

"I didn't know I had any."

"You don't have to be so defensive all of the time."

"I wouldn't be defensive if I wasn't feeling attacked."

"Then let me try to help. I don't want you to just lash out at-"

"I wasn't lashing out! I didn't attack anyone, I didn't "assault" anyone, I was just helping a friend, why is that so hard for everyone to understand? He tackled Will, I pushed him, he pushed me, he punched me, I threw him, it's not like he was some innocent party in all this!" I gestured upwards sharply and was thrown forward in my seat. The tires screamed, my seatbelt seized, and I felt a sharp thunk. My mother stared forward and tried to catch her breath, "Mom, are you okay? What did… we…" I looked ahead, and saw the asphalt raised in a sudden, short cliff. Water bubbled up out of the road. It must have broken a pipe. My mother's hands were shaking as she put the car in a slow reverse and sped off. There would be no way of explaining this to the authorities, especially not after today.

"Did I just…" The pause drew itself out, as neither of us had the nerve to speak for some time; I nodded slowly, and finally regained my verbal footing. "Psychologist… yeah… okay…"

Not another word was said, and made it the last six blocks home without further incident. She murmured something that I think was "good night" and went back to bed, but not to sleep. I was sure she tried to, but one quick read and I could tell she was still awake, and probably tossing and turning. I had cost her a day's sleep, but after the stance she had taken in this ordeal, I didn't feel guilty for it. I went to my room, lay down on my bed, and tried not to break anything until my father got home.

Her bedroom door opened as soon as the front door had, and she got to him first. I'm sure he was told the entire story over tea, which was also my mother's stressed out drink of choice. No one raised their voices, so I was left out of the ability to eavesdrop, but their concern hung in the air and dripped on everything nearby.

The school bus pulled up to our stop, paused, and moved on. I wondered how William was doing, usually by now the garage door was being flung open, and some band that broke up in 1974 was playing at as full of blast. Our home was quiet, and so was his, and I could feel its pressure weighing me down. It was suffocating, the house was cold and sterile, and in my mind I still felt the emotional storm drifting through the house.

I wanted to go back to yesterday, to being annoyed about the rain storm and how dull the grass still managed to be even though it was spring. I wanted to hear William's animated frustration at hard to reach bolts and scuffed up knuckles as he fought with his brother's car. Yesterday had been so much easier than today, and I hated myself for being underwhelmed by it. I didn't miss my old routine until it was pulled out from under me. The garage door never opened, the music never turned on. I stayed in bed until I was called for dinner, and afterwards went right back to it. I lay face down and wished all of this magic nonsense had never happened to any of us. I curled on my side as the unusual, unnatural lost feeling took me. I just wanted William and I to be normal boys…

I sat up in bed, and replayed my own thoughts. "Wait… what?" My brain and I needed to have a very serious conversation.

# Chapter Fourteen

I was up bright and early when I heard the garage door rise, and I threw on whatever pants were in reach and a shirt, scrambling through the dewy grass in my slippers. The toolbox rattled across Will's driveway, and I rushed to meet him.

"Nice pajama pants."

"Shut up," I said and hugged him. He blinked, and we both pulled back quickly. "How'd your evening go?" I asked, leaning on his brother's car.

"My mom wants to sue everyone from Mrs. Bridges up to the school system."

"Wow, she's sounding like a New England native already…"

"How was yours? Um, Abs, I need in there." He shooed me off the hood.

"My mom's sending me to a psychiatrist, and I'm suspended for two weeks."

"That's… fuck." He shook his head.

"Yeah, my thoughts exactly."

"Are you going to fail?"

"I don't know yet. Mom says I can go to summer school or something."

"Mom wants to home school me now or send me to private school somewhere. She thinks I won't be safe anymore."

"Dude, I want to be home schooled." I crossed my arms and remembered I had forgotten to put on a bra. Actually, I'd forgotten there was anything to restrain to begin with, but I kept my arms crossed for propriety's sake. The thoughts of last night rolled back into my head. "So, have you ever wanted to be a girl?"

William straightened up a bit, and ducked to not hit his head, "And the art of conversation derailing award goes to Abby…" I read him, he was somewhere between confused and amused, any of the muse words.

"Well?"

"No, I can't say I have. Wait, do you think I'm gay?" He went from 'mused to defensive.

"I was just curious."

"I'm not gay. Not that there's anything wrong with that, but I'm not."

"My mom thinks you are." I smirked, finally things were lightening up.

"So does mine!" He sighed, throwing up his hands, and accidentally threw the wrench across the lawn. There was another long pause.

"I kind of broke the car," I said, and looked over my shoulder at the dented Outback in our driveway.

"How? You can't even drive." He went looking for his wrench.

"I think… I made the road attack it."

He paused, still bent over, wrench in hand, and stood up. He arched a brow, "You made the road…attack it…so you have what, magical pothole abilities now, on top of asshole flinging? You witches have the weirdest powers."

"Oh says the were hare! Or is the proper term were bunny? Were rabbit? Werabbit…"

"Okay, if you don't have magical pothole powers, how did you hurt the car? It looks like your mom just hit another curb or bollard."

"Bol-what?"

"The concrete poles that make sure cars know their place." He gestured with the wrench and cast a wary gaze upon the Subaru. He looked back, "But seriously, Abs, how did you make the road attack the car?"

"It kind of jumped… like, separated and jutted up, like a bad earth-quake effect." I tried to T my hands together in a way to show what I meant.

"How in the hell did you do that?"

"I don't know, I just did."

"Did you…I don't know, report it?" Only Will would ask that question, he was more of a goody two-shoes than I was sometimes.

I was almost feeling guilty now, another mark had been added to my previously spotless criminal record. "No, it was a hit and run."

Will glanced over at me, "Are you sure you did it?" He gestured with the wrench, "It's not some weird Connecticut sinkhole activity?"

"It came up, not down, and yeah, I'm pretty sure. I was mad at the time, and I did this" I turned my palms up and pushed towards the sky, "And then it just happened."

Will looked from me, to the car, to the ground in front of me, "It didn't work." He nodded astutely.

"Well I wasn't trying this time. I'm not angry at anything; I'm mildly annoyed at the worst."

He smirked, "I can fix that."

"No need, I can handle it. Do you want me throwing things around again? I already broke one car—" I looked to his brother's Mustang. William looked deviously at it, and I sighed, rolling my eyes. "No."

"Where's your sense of adventure?"

"That's not adventure, it's vandalism. Besides, he gives us rides, and he's a nice guy and, you know." I was suddenly met with a very suspicious gaze. I sighed. "Will, I don't want your brother, he's just a cool dude."

"Don't remind me," William huffed, and slipped back under the hood. There was a long silence. I leaned on the side; I didn't have to try to do a reading to feel what he did. I rarely had to, much to my frustration. My mind wandered, to the day before, to this sudden manifestation of powers I never knew about, or wanted for that matter. I missed the days of only being able to fly. I smirked, and leaned around the hood, "Hey, you want to go do something?"

"What do you have in mind?"

# Chapter Fifteen

I held on tight to Will's waist, my cheek tucked into his shoulders, hiding my face from the world. I could feel his warm chest, and I squeezed tighter when I did. This could have almost been nice. It was nearly romantic, which I wasn't entirely opposed to. But right now, it was an act of survival against the cold and the wind.

I leaned over too close, and my helmet smacked against his with a plastic clack. The wind burned my cheeks, and Will's hair gave me a lashing across the face as it flew free. I let go of him just enough to tuck it into the collar of his leather jacket, and tried to find that warm place to spare my fingers. The leather gloves I wore were protective, I'd hopefully save my fingers in a crash, but they did almost nothing for the cold without a liner. The world's fastest weed whacker was making a horrific ruckus under me, and spewing a cloud of blue smoke behind us. We turned off down country road after country road, staying as out of sight in the countryside as we could. It wasn't as big of a deal in the summer, with scooters and bikes everywhere, but it wasn't entirely legal for me to be a passenger on a bike driven by a minor, even if he did have his full license. In this weather, we were already conspicuous enough, but the broom-stick strapped to my back would not help in our efforts to blend in.

We found a field, still grey and dead for the winter. The nearby woods had a reputation for being a 4-wheeling hangout, which meant they didn't worry too much about trespassing. It was technically illegal to ride anywhere but our own, personal property, but I needed to feel the earth fly by under me, and the wind at my face, and not just the wind of being a frigid passenger on a poorly planned March motorcycle ride.

"There's no one parked at the farm house!" William had to shout over the sound of the engine and the wind.

"Great!" I yelled back into his helmet where his ear should be. He pulled in on a long dirt access road, and we vanished out of view of the farm house behind a hill. All that stretched out ahead was the wintered field, and clumps and lines of trees. It was the only open, flat area for miles. We came to a stop, and I dismounted before he killed the engine. I unstrapped the broom, which had been held on with a haphazard harness of belts from my bedroom, the more delicate fine branch "bristles" had been wrapped up in a beach towel, I freed it carefully, and shook out the twigs. Will took the towel, spread it on the ground, and sat heavily. "I want a go, once you remember what you're doing, okay?" He looked hopefully up at me. I nodded, and zipped up my jacket.

"Goggles?" I held out a hand for them, and he pulled them off the top of his head. I mounted up, pulled my goggles down, and concentrated. A deep breath and I broke into the best duck-legged sprint I could, and jumped. The broom bucked sharply and twisted under me, and I lost my grip less than eight inches off the ground as it made a sharp pull up. As soon as I let go, it fell dead, and I landed sorely on my backside. My audience stifled a chuckle. I turned back the other way, and repeated, with similar results at about a foot and a half up this time.

"Not like riding a bike, eh?" he called.

"I can't do that either!"

"Seriously?"

"Stop distracting me!"

Another sprint, and another flop. I picked splinters out of the delicate parts of my jeans. "One more time!" I yelled at Will, who hadn't actually said anything, but I could feel his amusement. It was pissing me off. I turned, and aimed the tip of my broom off towards the horizon, and tried to envision flying. I pictured the ground under my feet, picking up speed, going higher and higher. My mind slipped away on me, and I once more saw myself falling, falling by the islands, with the body that was mine, yet not mine. I froze.

"Abs?"

I tried to focus on the one glimmer of hope in that dream. Our hands catching in mid-air, that brief moment of safety. I lingered on what I felt when I saw my hands, my limbs, all utterly alien, but my own. Something sparked. I broke into a run. I kicked off from the ground with every ounce of strength my muscles could command. My broom bucked and rolled in my grasp, and bowed itself upward, but I held on.

My leather gloves saved my fingers, as I held the shaft in a death-grip. I tucked into a jockey's curl, and shot towards the sky. The length of birch and willow had a life of its own, an untamed spirit I had woken again, something deep inside me was being stirred by force, and it didn't like it. I was thrown into an unintentional barrel roll and was sent hurtling towards the tree line, just barely curving it away, back towards the field. It shot skyward again, it wanted away from me.

"Stop!" I yelled at it, leaving the trees behind far below me.

It obeyed, and I was shooting back towards the ground. It rolled again suddenly, and I managed to twist it level. I was finally flying parallel to the ground, and tried desperately to recall how to steer it. Slowly, it came back to me, the idea of guiding it with my weight, and with my intention. I'd forgotten what I had learned when I was just four, not to pull it along, but to guide.

"Got it now Abs?" I heard him yell below me.

"I'm not dead yet!" I leaned over called down in my best bad English accent. I promptly did a roll, having utterly forgotten about the whole concept of weight distribution. I left out an embarrassing yelp and managed to get right side up after a bit of awkward scrambling. I could hear him laughing below me, and in a less than fully planned stunt, I turned the broom around and buzzed past his head.

William yelped and hit the ground, hands over his head. "Not funny Abs!"

I shouted back between laughs, "Plenty funny!" I took the broom and gave it another sharp corner as I flew up and up. I could see the farmhouse now, still vacant. Off in the distance was The Snip, a lake tucked high in the hills. I could just barely see the observation point on the nearby mountain ridge. I then realized that anyone else could probably see me, too. I rolled the broom gently, relaxed, and lazily spiraled towards the ground. I touched down, graceful for just a moment, then lost my footing in the mud and stumbled.

"Classy last maneuver there." William sat back on the towel I'd wrapped my broom in. "You think I can have a go yet?"

I struggled for breath. "Weres don't fly." I suddenly found myself exhausted now that my feet had touched the ground. My shoulders and chest muscles ached now that I had released the broom, and the insides of my knees felt bruised.

"I meant with you. You know, two up, like we do on the bike."

"Maybe next time."

"At this rate, next time will be when you're twenty-three."

Rather than be offended, I laughed. "You might be right!" I limped towards him. "I think I'm done for the day. I'm not sure I can do another round."

He gave me a quizzical look but nodded. "Yeah, all right. Next time." He turned towards the farm house behind the hill, and his eyes went wide. "Come on, wrap it up and get your gear." He dressed swiftly for his bike, and kick-started the engine into life.

I heard a car in the distance and the telltale plink-plink of gravel hitting the underside. The owners of the house were back. I hastily bound up my broom and belted it onto my back as quickly as I could.

Helmet, check. Jacket, Check. "Let's go." I gave Will the two-tap signal to show I was ready. The bike took off with a mighty whirr and a plume of blue smoke. We took the corner hard and skidded out of the driveway. The Vespa scrambled for grip, caught the pavement, and we shot off down the road.

My jacket shifted and settled as I tried to one-hand zip it up. It pulled tighter on me, and I felt something loosen and begin to slip. My mind was two steps behind the world, as I felt my broom slip out of its makeshift harness and catch the pavement. I clung suddenly to Will when I felt it pull me back.

The good news was I didn't fall, and I was relieved right up until I heard it snap. The pressure released suddenly, and the handle slid lifelessly out of its binds and clattered into the road. I nearly punched him in the gut as I signaled Will to stop. It felt like forever to another driveway to turn around, and as we pulled out to go back, a pickup truck went thundering by. The air jostled us, and the pavement was scattered with splinters.

We pulled to the side of the road, and silently gathered the bits and pieces into the dirty, damp towel. I found the largest piece halfway down a ditch embankment, a two foot end, blue ribbon loop still in fact through the tip. Will jerked me out of the way as someone laid on the horn and swerved, grinding the remaining pieces into mulch. I bundled its remains, cradling the towel in my lap as we rode back. No words were exchanged; I held on limply and rest my cheek on his shoulder the whole return trip. The wind and lashings of hair didn't seem like much right now. The end on the loop dangled from my wrist, blowing in the wind and striking my thigh. I let it; it would be the last time my broom ever got to fly.

"Where have you been all day?" were my father's words as I had tried to slip in the garage side door.

"Out with Will." I found my voice was barely there anymore, my arms still wrapped protectively around that dirty, damp towel.

"What have you got there?" He looked up from the pot he had been stirring.

I bit my lip, and inhaled. My breath was stolen away by a silent sob, and I shut my eyes tight. I tried to summon something, anything, some kind of response to pacify him so that I could slip away to my room.

He saw the loop hanging, and he dropped his spoon into the pot. "Oh Pumpkin…" He hugged me tight, and petted my hair, even with sweaty helmet head.

"I screwed up… it fell… it's…" Words failed me utterly as I finally broke down sobbing. I found little comfort in his hug; I wanted to vanish from the world right at that moment.

"Do you want me to wake your—?"

I tensed and pulled back. "No!" It came out more forceful than I had intended.

He looked stunned a moment. Then, he nodded slowly. "Okay. I'll call you when dinner's ready. Get me if you need something, okay, Pumpkin?"

I nodded, and was hugged against my will. I let it go, and went numbly back to my room. There was nowhere to go from here. I gingerly set the bundle of twigs and splinters on my desk. I shut the door, and looked at the hook where it had always hung. Carefully, I put my broom back in its place. And now, two feet of birch hung from the hook on my door. I fell back into bed, and surrendered to the mess of feelings that had been threatening to burst out.

It was like being hit by a train.

# Chapter Sixteen

I was falling again. I stretched out my hand below me, and saw the long, bony, awkward arm of the last falling dream. It was alien, but familiar, and it was mine. A floating island drifted aside and clipped my shoulder. I cried out, and the surface gave way, and I was falling again. I grabbed at my shoulder, and felt my arm sink against my chest. I managed to look down, or maybe up with the angle I was taking. My shirt billowed and flapped, and I saw nothing there but smooth, flat pink skin. I wasn't a girl. It was startling enough to make me forget I was falling to my death.

For a moment, anyway.

I tried to shift and maneuver, and right myself to at least land on my feet if I had the opportunity. The wind encircled me, I could no nothing to slow my fall, only brace for impact if something chose to hit me. I was hurtling towards another island, a massive weeping cheery tree grew in the center, and even as I approached, the air was filled with pink petals. A noise echoed, a dull, hollow rapping.

"Aaron!"

I looked for her voice. It was second nature; it had always been my name. The ground came rushing at me, and instead of snapping my legs on impact, I slowed at the last moment, and touched down. My bare feet laced into the soft, turquoise grass. It was warm on my soles. I stared up in wonder at the great weeping cheery, a plume of pink fluff and ornate, winding coils. It was like a willow, my "blessing sign," but different. These trees started their lives pink, and fluffy, but in the end were just like any other cherry.

"Aaron!" she called again. And then, I saw her. The hazel-eyed girl was bounding towards me. Her dress flowed around her, and she gracefully swam in its slowed ripples. It followed her body like the trailing fins of a fish. "I missed you!" She threw her arms around my neck and tucked her cheek against mine.

"Abigail, wake up!" My mother was nearly shouting through my bedroom door, "You're going to be late!"

"I don't have school, Mom!" My voice was not the one I was expecting. It was a shrill, nasal whine.

"Your psychiatrist appointment is in an hour!"

I sat up and tried to orient myself. "Yes Mom."

There was no time to try to reconcile with this body, and I dressed it in a rush. I went to open my door and saw the broken broom handle hanging there. It had been there two days now, and it still stole my breath when I saw it.

My mother looked me over and pulled a stray hair off my shirt. "You're a mess."

"It's a shrink, not a job interview." I wanted to get some sort of breakfast before we had to leave.

"At least brush your hair. Honestly, you're nothing like most girls your age."

She had no idea how right she was. I brushed it, begrudgingly and vocally as the brush caught every knot, snag, and deviant curl. I was adamant in my pursuit of something to eat, and settled on one of Laurie's blueberry toaster pastries. It tasted like sugar and crumbly clay, with a dose of fake blueberry, but right now it was the most delicious fake blueberries and clay.

"There are crumbs on your shirt." My mother went to brush them off for me, and I dodged and did so myself. She was pacing, with her car keys in hand but no coat on yet. "Are you ready yet? "

I poured and just as quickly downed a glass of orange juice, then nodded. I fetched my coat, and buttoned it up tight. My hands felt small, and my body was excessively padded all over. The coat wasn't helping matters at all, adding an extra cushioned inch to, well, everything. I watched trees go by, and become fewer and fewer as we got closer to Hartford.

"I bet Will can fix the bumper." The silence was killing me after fifteen minutes.

"He's not a mechanic."

"He built his bike, and he fixes everything else within reach."

"We'll take it to a body shop, Abby."

"But he's probably cheaper and just as good."

"He's a nice boy, but he's still just a kid with a wrench. It needs to go to a professional."

I sighed, and leaned on the arm rest on my door. She was wasting her money. I felt like saying the guy at the shop would probably be a kid too, just be six months older and with less experience. The country roads were long behind us, and the world was one big traffic jam. The architecture was a mismatched jumble of modern high rises and colonial buildings, speckled with monuments and 400 year old cemeteries.

"You couldn't find someone in Rockville? Or Enfield?"

"She has a very good reputation, and she knows how to deal with people like you, or rather, us."

I withheld the sarcastic comment that bit at my tongue. "I see. So she knows magical types?" I waved my hand airily.

"Yes. They're one of her specialties."

"Do you think this will actually help?"

"I hope so." Her tone was less than optimistic, and not the response I was looking for. We parked on the street, and my mom fed the meter. We weren't far from a park; I could see green trees peeking out here and there. It was almost heartening to have that little dose of nature in the ravine of concrete and stone.

"Come on."

I hadn't realized I'd just been standing there staring at trees, and shuffled along after my mother. She checked me in, and we waited. I played with my phone, and sent Sylvia a text.

**[Help. I'm in the shrink's office.}**

A few minutes later, in the middle of a game, I got a response.

**{Sounds about right.]**

I didn't get to send another before my name was called, and I went scuttling along back down the hallway. A thick woman with a black bun and thick rimmed "trendy" glasses let me in. She looked a bit old to be a hipster, but it worked in a kind of cute librarian sort of way. "Have a seat, Abigail." She smiled warmly, and gestured to a wing-back chair that must have been stolen from some grandmother's house. It was classy, but dated, especially the green plaid. She sat across from me in her own, it looked like leather.

"So I don't get one of those fainting lounges?"

"Sorry, I'm afraid I just have chairs. I can get you a folding one if you don't like that one, or there's the one behind my desk." Another wing-back, this time on wheels, and a white and blue floral pattern. It looked even more like it had been stolen from some poor old lady.

"This one's fine. It's just… tall." I leaned back in it a bit, "But comfy." There was a pause; it felt like forever, like she was taking notes on my silence. "So what do we talk about?"

"Anything you want, Abby. Whatever is on your mind."

She gave me that warm smile again, and I felt suspicious. "Aren't you going to ask me about my mother or something? Say "Tell me about your childhood, Abigail" and then deduce that I have a crush on my dad or something else absurd like that?"

She laughed, but it didn't feel like she was laughing at me. "I can promise psychology has changed a lot since then. We don't just assume everyone is fixated on their mothers or has some sort of complex. Most of my clients are very normal people, and I just help them with their problems."

"I'm not very normal." I gave her a warning look.

She closed her eyes and smiled. She reminded me of a cat when she did that, one of those beckoning statues from Japan. "And what makes you think you're not normal, then?"

"Because my best friend is a rabbit, and I can evidently throw things with my mind. And I can fly around on a broomstick. Well, I could."

"Could you now? Why not anymore?"

"I broke it."

"That's terrible, did something happen?"

She gently herded me into explaining everything, and for once, I genuinely did not feel interrogated when an adult was asking me questions. Sometimes she wrote things down, and I would shut up for a moment and do my best to picture what she had said. Less than a week ago, I learned I had telekinesis, and I was hoping maybe I'd suddenly sprout telepathy too. No such luck. She always managed to get me talking again, and took her notes more discreetly now. I told her about my broom, about Will, about sneaking off to go flying.

"So what's school like?"

"I don't know, I'm not there." I paused my stream of consciousness babbling. "You were told to ask that, weren't you?" I sat up a bit straighter in my chair, having started to give in to its comforting plaid charm, and plush stuffing.

"No, not at all. School's a big thing for people your age; you spend a lot of time there."

"Well, physically. Mostly I just kind of clock out, pass the tests, and go home."

"What about your friends there?"

"I don't really have any. I have some, I don't know…acquaintances?"

"You don't have any school friends?"

"No, just my neighbor. I talk to a few people, like, I know their names, mostly anyway. They'll say hi or gossip at me a bit. I think they think we're friends."

"But you don't consider them friends?"

"No, we just kind of talk if we're bored. They're not people I'd share secrets with or even go hang-out with outside of school. I mean, they're nice, but we don't really mesh on any level. They're all about guys and new phones and celebrities who are in love and suddenly out of love, and it all just feels like parakeet chatter to me. We can't even really talk phones because I want to talk about clock speed and they're just twittering on about how shiny the newest Apple thing is and how it has all sorts of useless features or is a gnat's weight smaller."

"So you don't feel matched intellectually?"

"It's not that, I don't feel smart. I feel damned-er, sorry, darn stupid next to Will, and even dumber if he has a car nearby. It's not like I'm in advanced placement anything. I mean, I don't know, I guess I could be if I tried."

"Do you want to be in advanced classes?"

I shut up for the first time in ten minutes. "I don't know. I don't like homework, and I don't really have any college plans in mind. I mean, I guess I'll go, but I'm not shooting for the Ivy leagues, or even UConn. I mean, I probably should try for advanced classes, I know it would look good on applications and help better my future, but I guess…" I trailed off, and sighed. "I guess I'm just lazy."

"You sound like you're in need of direction, and maybe you don't know what you want to be yet."

I shifted uncomfortably, tucking into the corner of the monolith chair. She'd hit that one right on the head, but she didn't look smug about it at all. She gave me that same, friendly, cat like smile. I tried to relax again.

"I have no idea what I want to be, at all."

"Have you talked with a counselor at school?"

"No, I kind of lost faith after that career placement test that told me I should be either a nurse or a flower arranger."

She laughed a little, "And I take it neither of those interest you."

"I'm allergic, and I don't really like girly things."

"Nurse can be a unisex job." It was the first, minor bit of confrontation I had heard, I was almost grateful for it, it made her sound human. At least she felt less like a yes man now.

"That's true. I just don't think of it as one. And it doesn't really interest me."

"So what does interest you?"

She had me cornered; there wasn't really a dignified way out of this. I squirmed visibly, and tucked my hands under my thighs. "Video games, the internet; I liked some of the programming I did in class, that was fun. I like making websites. I read. I take photos and I guess I did photography club for a while until it was cut." I slumped a bit. I was pathetic; I had no future ambitions what so ever, I just liked playing with gadgets and escaping too far off worlds that were a lot more interesting than here. I looked up expecting a judgmental gaze, waiting to see her scowling and scribbling furiously at her notebook.

She just smiled. "That's very common for people your age. It can be a lot of pressure to figure out everything you want to do in life in the first sixteen years of it. Sometimes it takes time, especially if you've been depressed about something."

"I don't feel depressed." I leaned back in the chair again.

"I never said you were, but it's common to have problems like that if you are, especially if you haven't been sleeping well. Have you been sleeping? At least eight hours a night not just in class." She chuckled and covered her lips with her fingers, and looked even more like a beckoning cat than when she just smiled. "Dream-walking and Astral projecting don't count either."

"Kind of. I have weird dreams a lot, and sometimes they wake me up. And I can't astral project. What's dream walking?"

"It's an obscure technique, where you can communicate with others in dreams. It induces a light sleep, and it's interesting to try, but it's not very restful, and it only works between magic-blooded individuals."

"No, I can't do that either. Just fly brooms and throw things."

"Telekinesis is rather rare, especially in witches. But, back to your dreams, what are they like?"

"I'm falling. I'm surrounded by floating islands, and they're flying past me. It's like the planets in The Little Prince, but they have dirt underneath them. I'm always falling past them, and sometimes I hit one, and I can never get a good grip. Sometimes I meet a girl there."

"Is she someone you know?"

"No, I've never seen her before. She caught me, once. And then once I landed on her island, too."

"Is it the same girl every time?"

"Yeah, every time. So what does it mean?"

"What do you think it means?"

"You can't interpret my dreams?"

"Well, I can, but most dream interpretation is best done internally. I can tell you're not feeling secure. It's usually associated with anxiety or feeling out of control of a situation, and sometimes it's tied to a lack of identity."

I tensed, fearing she knew the part of the dream I withheld.

"But I think we both already knew that was a concern, and it's a very common one for a lot of teenagers. There's so much coming at you, and you're about to make a huge change, and it can be a frightening one. I can't really tell you specifics of what dreams mean, I won't tell you that white roses symbolize loss of innocence, or that the moon means your mother, none of it's quite that concrete. But, I can help guide you, so you can figure them out for yourself. Who knows what the moon means for you."

"Usually it means it's night time."

She laughed, and that simple action warmed up the room. I let my shoulders drop again, and exhaled, grinning a bit.

She checked her watch. "Well, we'll have to talk more about your dreams next time, especially if they're keeping you from sleeping. Sleep is critical at your age, you know. Oh! I have some papers for you to take home, and finish for our meeting next Tuesday."

"Wait, I have homework? For therapy?"

"You'll be surprised how fast you go through them." She went to her desk and started shuffling in a file with my name on it. I had missed it, just lying there the whole time. She handed them to me. "There are also some tips on helping to focus and get motivated on things. It's a common issue to have at your age even if you're well."

"I really have homework?"

"And I expect you to have it done."

"Wait… can I flunk out of therapy, too?" And this time I think she was laughing at me. But then again, I laughed too.

# Chapter Seventeen

I laid in bed, and waited. I was up much too early again, after another weird dream. I was listening for the familiar sound of the weed whacker firing up. Will was late, the sun was up and I couldn't hear him out tinkering with something. I looked to my broom, and sighed. The sting wasn't as strong anymore; it was a dull ache of melancholy. I didn't feel the same kind of bonded sadness, like some witches did. My mother had been worried after it was destroyed, afraid this was going to teeter off of some ledge she seems to think I'm sitting on. It wasn't like the loss of a friend, more like I had broken something irreplaceable. It wasn't even like it felt like it was mine. Worst of all, it came with an intense feeling that I had once again failed to be what I was supposed to be. I tried just once more to be a good witch, something I was never very keen on anyway, and what did I do? I broke the only tie I had left. It had become a physical reminder of just how bad I was at this.

William still wasn't up, or maybe he just wasn't out yet. He always woke before the sun, before everyone else in his house. I wondered if it was pathetic that I was basing all of my time around when I would get to see him.

My phone buzzed beside me, and I opened the unread email. I had poured my heart out on Sylvia a few days ago, and told her everything. I told her about Will's shift, my suspension, destroying me broom, and even my new therapist. I even told her about my dreams. She was in a traditional studies program in Pennsylvania; I had hoped she maybe knew a little about dream interpretation, that wasn't just "it is what you make it." Her response was short, mostly sympathetic, and a little condescending in a way that I probably deserved. Even I knew I had screwed up, multiple times, or more like repeatedly. The last part of her email was what concerned me.

Are you always a boy when you dream?

I stared at the screen a long while, and flopped heavily back into the bed again. I sprawled a bit, and tried to think. I didn't recall my dreams often; it was part of why the constant falling and "Little Prince" islands stuck out to me. Usually, they were purely surreal, like taking a road trip with a talking jackrabbit and my gym teacher, the needing to deliver a blessed roast chicken to the village of the cactus people. They were also usually gone within minutes of waking up.

I couldn't remember the last time I dreamed I was a girl, at least obviously one. Usually I never saw myself, so I just assumed I was probably one. I guess it never occurred to me to look down and check, when I was on the quest for the purple peacock of wisdom in the land of giant frogs. I chewed my lip, sighed, and picked up the phone again.

*No, I'm always a boy now. I never think of myself as a girl, I'm just whatever I am.*

I didn't expect a text less than five minutes later, and was startled by my phone's frantic buzzing. I was half-asleep when it had struck, having vibrated and bumbled into my cheek.

**{Do you feel like a boy when you're not asleep?]**

**[How do you feel like a boy, anyway? I don't feel like a girl, but I'm not a good example of the breed.}**

**{Point. But do you wish you were one? Do girl things feel weird?]**

**[Girl things have always felt weird. I think that's normal. I don't know if I wish I was one. I don't like being a girl, though. I don't feel like anything.}**

**{What about your girly parts?]**

I stared at the phone judgmentally. I couldn't believe she was really asking that kind of thing, or even talking about that. It felt rude. The phone buzzed a moment later.

**{Maybe not like THAT but, the girl parts of your body?]**

I waited, and pondered. I rolled over, and felt everything shift in the same, old, somewhat alien way. I was so used to every part of me feeling awkward, squishy, and misshapen that It had never even occurred to me that this might not be normal. That lingering darkness was suddenly making sense. It was how I had felt ever since puberty hit me like a brick. I just assumed that someday, everything would feel right, and my body and I would make peace. I was still waiting for that, I had been clinging to the idea that I was a late bloomer, and it would suddenly all make sense.

**{Abby?]**

**[Sorry. Yeah, I don't like those.}**

**{I was reading you all weekend, you know. It was a weird aura. You felt like a friend of mine.]**

**[Is she crazy too?}**

**{No, she's transgender.]**

I stared at that last word. I tried to swallow around the lump in my throat, and my hands started to shake. I put my phone down. I picked it back up, and hurled it into my closet.

I wanted to bury it away under my remaining shreds of girly clothes. I wanted to smother it in skirts and purple socks, because it was lying to me. I rolled over and covered my head in the pillow, and did what felt right. I screamed. I cursed; I let out more fucks than I had ever done in my life. I clung to it, and screamed again. She was lying. She was wrong. I wasn't like that. I couldn't be like that!

Tears streamed down my face, and I had no idea where they came from. I couldn't even describe what I was feeling; my world was caving in around me. I refused to be one of those freaks, I was a girl dammit. "I'm a fucking girl!" I screamed into the pillow. Sobs stole control of me, and each breath was a painful, gagging shudder. My phone rang, somewhere in the dark confines of my closet. I let it go to voicemail. I couldn't bring myself to answer it, not like this. I got another text afterwards. And another. I hated that thing. I hated Sylvia. She was wrong, absolutely wrong.

This couldn't be happening to me.

## Chapter Eighteen

I got up, eventually, and dressed. Sports bra, hoodie, cargo pants, hat, it would do. I went over to Will's house, and knocked lightly at the garage door. I didn't want to wake the entire house. Nothing. I heard a noise, something was thunking about in there. "Mr. Mr. and Mrs. Lagai?" Nothing. Something was definitely in there. I tried to pull the door up from the handle, and it stuck. "Brian? Um… Badger? It's just me, Abby." I could hear what almost sounded like scampering. Maybe they had a raccoon, or their cat got locked in again.

I circled around to the back yard, tried the lock, and jumped the fence. They always left their back door into the garage open, most people didn't risk the dog that was usually in the yard. A hundred and forty pounds of German shepherd barked and went lunging after me. She tackled, and stuck her nose in my eye, and slurped. "Hi Camile." I rubbed her neck and tried to navigate to the door and juggle the dog. "Cammy, down." She licked my hands and stuffed her nose in my pockets, grunting and groaning as I forced her down on all fours again. "There's an intruder in your garage, Cammy!" I pointed at the door. She wagged. "Well, some guard dog you are." I picked up a tennis ball of distraction +2, and hurled it to the far end of the yard. She galloped that way, and I slipped into the garage. "Hello?" The light was on, there were some tools on the floor. "Will?" Something darted in my periphery. "Kitty Kitty?" I called hesitantly. It wasn't a kitty, but a rabbit shot out from under a rolling tool chest. I shut the door quickly, and sighed. "Oh Will…" I found his clothes near the door to the house and just waited, watching the rabbit go bouncing from corner to corner, sniffing things, pulling over bins, and chew on the edge of a screwdriver. "Will, no!" I shooed him away, and picked up the tools. He wouldn't stay shifted long, he never did. I waited with his pants in hand. He turned back suddenly; it wasn't the long, drawn out process of old monster movies. At least, it wasn't anymore for him. He was past the days of slow, awkward shifts, but not quite able to control them. I looked away quickly and shielded my eyes. "Catch." I threw his pants his way, and waited as I heard him dress. I peeked out between my fingers, to verify that he was decent now.

"So, what brought that on?"

He didn't answer right away, sitting heavily on the bench along the wall. He was out of breath. "I… don't remember. Bad night of sleep, and a… stressful morning."

"Stressful?"

"Don't wanna talk about it…" We sat in silence, as my friend gathered his strength. I did the same, in a different way. I still didn't know what to make of what happened an hour ago, but I was out of tears. It was seven in the morning, and I had run out of energy.

"Want some coffee? Or tea?"

"Tea…" He trailed off, seeming lost in thought a moment, "Tea would be nice."

I handed him his shirt and jacket, and he followed me barefoot through the cold grass. We settled in my kitchen. He sat at the bar-top counter, and I got the kettle going. It was a symbiotic silence, as we found calm just in the presence of each other. I fished in the cabinet, and pulled us each out a bag of Earl Grey. I spooned sugar into the bottom of the mugs. He took my arm in passing, as I shifted to the counter. "Thanks Abs…" He murmured. His hands were warm, and for a moment he seemed to lean on my arm, taking in a breath and exhaling slowly. And then, he let go, and that moment was over.

"Don't mention it." I tripped over the words, and for once found myself admiring something about him that wasn't just brains or ambition. I took in the whole feeling that was my best friend, and read a gentle, warm, yet exhausted aura that poured off him. It was like steam. The kettle started to sing, the momentary low whistle before it would start to scream. I scrambled to pull back the whistler tip before the whole house woke up, and let it boil uncapped. I poured a mug for each of us, and sat at the counter next to him.

"Come here often?" I grinned at him. He chuckled, and gave me the suggestive eyebrow wiggle. The feelings of a moment ago had dissipated, or perhaps I just didn't feel able to wrangle them this morning. He was my friend, my best friend. And besides, he didn't like boys.

A few jokes and gentle ribbing held the creeping, dark sensation at bay. It had seized me by force, but Will had stolen me back. Soon, I was okay again. I was confused as hell, about everything, from what I was, to what I felt, but I was still somehow okay. I was going to survive the day, and maybe I'd manage to talk to Syl again. I didn't know what was right, but I was at least feeling ready to face whatever it was.

I turned to my lanky best friend; a question had been nagging me all morning. Well, most of it. "So, what made you change anyway?"

"A horrible night's sleep. On the couch in the family room."

"What on earth were you doing out there? Brian's' snoring that bad?"

"No, not exactly. He had…" Will trailed off. His cheeks flushed all the way into his ears, and he talked into his teacup. "He had company last night."

"Oh… Oh!" I looked away. "I get it, he snuck a girl over and you got banned to the couch all night."

"Not exactly…"

"He didn't sneak her over?"

"No, it wasn't a girl."

I had no idea how to respond to that, at all. I drank my tea with purpose now, because it bought me some extra silence to think this over. The star stag of the track team had jumped the fence. It didn't look like Will knew what to make this either.

"There's… nothing wrong with that. Kind of, well, I mean he shouldn't be sneaking anyone over, but it's okay that he's…"

"Yes, I know. There's nothing wrong with that. But… But he's my brother. It's weird. I see him flirt up every girl that looks his way at school, but he's been seeing Chad since like, sophomore year."

"So all those girls he's been out with?"

"Just friends, Or a cover, or… I don't know, it pisses me off that he does it."

"And you knew?"

"Yep."

"What do your parents think?"

"They have absolutely no idea. They haven't even met Chad; I think he was over to study twice."

"Wow. I mean, what would they do?"

"I don't know. I don't think he knows. They act like they're okay with all of that, my dad has even handled a few discrimination cases. But, he's family. He's the oldest son and they expect him to go to college and have two point five kids and live in some three bedroom house with the perfect wife and be a rocket scientist."

I nodded, taking another long drink of tea. Then, I blinked, the gears were turning in my head. "Wait, you mean Chad Deban? Computer club Chad? Makes apps in his sleep Chad?" I had been to a few meetings of the computer club, but never had reliable transport after school unless I wanted to walk four miles every Tuesday and Friday.

"Yeah. That Chad."

"Well fuck… no wonder Brian's suddenly passing Calculus."

Will broke down laughing, after flooding his sinuses with tea. He sputtered and coughed, and I offered him a napkin from the chrome diner-style dispenser we had. He didn't get his breath again for a while, and the ruckus had caused a stirring in the rest of the house. My dad shuffled out in his bath robe and plaid pajama pants. "Oh, morning you two." He looked baffled to see two fully dressed teenagers sipping tea and up bright and early before even the birds were awake.

"We got cold working on the car." I cradled my teacup for warmth. Will did the same rather quickly, and luckily his blush could pass for chill.

"Mmmhm…" He didn't look concerned by us. He was much more bothered with getting the stovetop espresso pot going. "You two want some coffee?"

"We have tea, but thank you sir." said William, smiling with a sudden, almost dynamic sort of warm cheer.

My dad didn't notice, he just nodded, "Okay then…"

"Come on Will. Let's get out of his hair." We went to my room. Will sat on my bed, I leaned on the desk.

"Won't your parents, you know, mind us being alone in here?" Usually we hung out in the living room.

"Nah, they trust us."

Will paused, and sighed, "Do they think I'm gay, too?"

"And will support you no matter what, since you're practically a member of the family."

"Dammit. They got the wrong boy." He flopped back on my bed, almost spilling the mug of tea he seemed to forget he had. My phone chirped and buzzed in the closet, and I scrunched a bit at its ruckus. I wished it would shut it already and leave me in peace, like the device itself was antagonizing me, and not the person on the other end.

"Another early bird?" Will asked, trying to drink and lay down.

"My cousin. We were messaging each other this morning."

"You actually talk to family again?"

"Yeah, didn't I tell you? We got reacquainted at the family reunion, when my creepy little cousin got her broom." I looked sadly at mine. "It's kind of weird, she's a year older than me, and she's married and has a kid now and everything. She's in a magical studies program."

"That is weird. I think I'd break a kid, I can barely handle Camile, and she at least knows where to crap."

"Brynn's not bad. She's like a familiar right now. I think they have a psychic link or something."

"Do witches usually do that with babies?"

"I don't know. Never been interested in one enough to ask. It's just weird that she's already an adult with a family and a house, and I don't even know if I want to go to college, or what I want to do in the long run. I mean, I like some stuff, but it's not career stuff. I don't think the world needs space marines yet, or crowbar wielding physicists to help save the world."

"Yeah, professional gamer is only really a career in South Korea."

I laughed, almost choking on my tea.

"But you would make a great space marine. I could definitely see that. Real marine? Less so." Will nodded. His eyebrows arched up, and he seemed to get it. "So what you mean is you just have no idea what to do with your life."

"Bingo."

"And let me guess, you've been sitting back and waiting for something interesting to happen that will get your ass in gear and then you'll actually know what you're doing and it will all be kittens, sunshine and success?"

"There is no need to be a jerk about it…"

"But am I right?"

"Yes, and I hate you. I mean, who doesn't want to suddenly realize what they want to do forever and actually get paid for it? I'd love to find out what clicks and be set to go forth and do what I love, but everything I love is just a hobby, or I'm too lazy to actually make anything out of it. I mean, I learned a ton of Java in two weekends, and then instead of deciding to do something useful, I sat on my butt and killed virtual dragons for six weeks straight. I can't even remember most of last November because all I did was play that stupid game."

"Pre-ordered the expansion?"

"Yes and shut up. That's not the point." I glared at him. He didn't notice, he was staring at my ceiling and still trying to drink tea horizontally.

"So you're like basically every person ever and enjoy your hobbies more than working? Is that what you're trying to get at?" He would have sounded a lot wiser through all of this if he weren't constantly pouring Earl Grey on his face as he tried to drink sideways.

"What I'm getting at is that I don't know what I want to do with myself, at all. I feel like everyone else has taken off around me and found their true calling, and I'm still sitting here waiting for my life to actually feel like mine. I feel like I'm waiting for something to happen, and I'll finally turn into what I'm supposed to be. And then I'll know what I want to do, and who I am, and it will be sunshine and unicorns and kittens and rainbows."

"You'll figure it out eventually, everyone does. I mean, it's kind of stupid that we're forced to pick our career paths for life before some of us can even drive. I'm too young to go buy a cigarette, but I'm expected to know what I want to do for the rest of my life and get a head start on it? I don't even know what I want for lunch most days."

"I guess you're right. I mean, I wouldn't trust most of the people my age to know how to pick a practical shoe out and not screw it up."

"Steel toe, good brand, re-soleable, genuine leather."

"Damn it Will, stop being perfect at everything." I set my teacup down with a resonating thunk. He jumped, and spilled his. I gave him a smug look, "Well, almost everything."

He huffed and was quiet for a bit. I thought he was trying to glue his dignity back together. "But anyway, you don't have to be ready for everything yet. You still have one more year, and at least eight months before you really have to buckle down for college applications. So don't worry about it. It wouldn't even kill you to take a year off if you need it, so long as that doesn't mean you just spend a year killing dragons and aliens. Maybe you need to, and this sounds really, really new agey and like movie Indian bullshit, but maybe you need to go out and find yourself."

"That did sound really hippy."

"Shut up, I'm trying to help and you know it. Geeze, give you a hand, and you bite mine."

"Did not."

"Did too." He sat up and glared at me.

I backed off and finished the last of my tea."Sorry man, didn't mean to." I shrugged.

He waved airily and fell back with an audible sort of "whump," making my stray socks go airborne before landing back on the bedspread. "It's cool." My phone threw another fit in my closet, screaming for attention like an impatient child. "You can get that if you want to."

"It can wait. It feels rude to talk to a far away person when you have a live one captive."

"You sound like my dad."

"And your dad is super polite and likeable. He rolled a twenty when he was doing his Charisma score."

"Touché. Speaking of, bug your dad, I want to play again. It's been months."

"I'll do that. He's been busy at work, so I think he forgot the campaign again." I laughed, "Laurie's teacher was worried that he was drawing devils in class, my dad had to explain what a Kobold was."

"Start them young, and they will be awesome." Will did his best wise old sage voice.

I could hear Laurie was up now, which meant I had missed Mom coming home from work. My parents didn't see each other much until the evenings, Dad worked normal office hours, and Mom took the graveyard shift at the hospital. I didn't know how they could handle it, I'd go nuts if I had to be away from the person I was married to for that long. The high school bus went by. "When are you going back, anyway?"

"Back?"

"To school, bunny boy."

"Oh, next Monday. My mom is still on the war path. She wants to pull me out so that I can go to a private school or shift to being home schooled so I can finish the year in peace. I know I was thrown under the social bus, but I don't think my life is going to be that screwed over. It's not like I'm dangerous or anything. I'm just a stupid rabbit."

I shrunk and pulled my shoulders in. I hadn't thought much about going back. Two weeks felt like it could be forever, and as always, I had put it out of mind. Will wasn't dangerous, but I was. At least on paper, I was. I wasn't sure how I would go back this year.

"How long have you got?"

I shrugged, "The week after you, I think. The school said they would call."

"Has my mom offered to sic our lawyer on them on your behalf too?"

"Probably. She hasn't told me much about her interactions with the school admin in this whole fiasco. I think she's afraid I'll freak out and break more stuff."

"Yeah, I could see that as being a problem."

"Jerk."

## Chapter Nineteen

I went back to my therapist four days after I first saw her. I even did my homework, which was evidently a first because my mother kept saying how she honestly just couldn't believe it. "Your faith in me is astonishing." And then I got a lecture. I mostly tuned her out as we waited by the front desk. It was almost like a doctor's office but with warmer colors on the wall and expensive grown-up magazines. I played games on my phone, since I had no interest in learning how to make "The Perfect Easter Centerpiece" or "How to Quadruple your Investment in Ten Years." I knew that either of these bits of knowledge would probably be more useful than another round of falling, colorful blocks set to Russian folk music, but the game made me happy. Briefly, that is. Was I really this lazy all the time? Did I do nothing but play stupid games and completely miss any opportunity to actually learn something?

I picked up the business magazine and turned to page eighty-one. I put it back down when the first three paragraphs made no sense whatsoever. I picked up a gentleman's magazine instead. An actual gentleman's magazine, not the kind with swimsuit models on the cover that comes wrapped in plastic. By the time my name was called, I knew twelve new ways to tie a scarf and signs that my carburetors need re-etted. Take that, brain, I learned something.

Soon I was back in the tacky yet friendly plaid chair. I handed my papers to the catlike woman, and she smiled and gave them a quick looking over. We discussed some of the same things as last time, in more detail. Mostly it involved my nervousness about the future, and my lack of security in knowing where I was going. I didn't know who I was, what I was, or where I was going. She assured me this was a common problem, and for once, I started to believe her.

"Many people your age are very insecure about their identities. And it's a time when you learn a lot about yourself. Sometimes you even change who you are entirely over the course of high school. It can be a jarring process."

My mind wandered when she mentioned changing identities. I thought back on the conversation I had left hanging with Sylvia. The dreams went racing through my head, replaying all at once, and in my mind, I was surrounded by monitors all screaming one message at me. You are not a girl.

She lowered her notebook, still awaiting some sort of response from me. She looked back at it, and jotted something down.

"Is that a common feeling you have, Abigail?"

"What?"

"The feeling that you don't know what you are, and should be something else." She gave me a very careful look.

I sat upright in my chair, "Yeah, I guess." I tried to sound casual and nonchalant about it. "You said it was common."

"A certain degree of a lack of identity is common, yes. However, I want to talk about what you just felt, right now."

"You mean not knowing what I want to be when I grow up?" I responded a lot more sarcastically then I had intended to. I shrunk, and immediately felt bad for it.

"No, I mean the feeling you felt right now. Like something wasn't quite right. Has it been going on long?" She was leading me around the subject, or maybe she wanted me to just admit it to her. I tried to read her and got static.

I braced myself in my chair. "It's been years now. It didn't used to be this bad. But the more I see other people settle into their roles, and the more I change, the worse it gets. I've been changing in the corner of the locker room since middle school, because I know something isn't quite right with me." I hoped she would give me some nugget of calming wisdom, or even a simple "That's perfectly normal." Instead, she just nodded, and took down a few notes.

"Do go on. If you feel comfortable, I'd like to hear more."

I sighed, and I found myself becoming much smaller in my seat. I was almost hugging my knee now; I wanted distance between the two of us. I wasn't on guard any more, I was scared. "It's been almost unbearable this last year. I can't shake it; the littlest things set it off. I wear sports bras because my arms brushing my chest feels alien. I shower in the dark, because I can't stand what I see. I don't connect with girls, at all. They're almost a foreign species to me. I've told my mom some of this before, a few times, and she just keeps telling me that this is all normal for my age and that it will go away soon. I want it to. I keep waiting for when I can just wake up and suddenly be okay with the fact that I'm going to spend the rest of my fucking life as a girl. I want to be okay with what I am, I want that more than anything, but it just keeps getting worse. I don't want to be a witch, or a girl, or whatever the hell I am. I just want to wake up tomorrow and be—."

I stopped, something was shaking, and I was having trouble breathing. I thought I was drowning for a moment, and realized I was crying. I was shivering. She didn't give me the cat-like smile this time. She nodded, and looked to be thinking. She handed me a box of tissues. It wasn't like the movies, where I could take one and dab my eyes. I'd overflowed her wastebasket, and I still couldn't calm my hands down when I finally settled in again. I wrapped myself around the blue floral print box, waiting for my emotions to betray me and explode again.

"I always dream I'm a boy. Every single time that I can remember. I want to be normal, and be okay with what I am, but it's just not working. I've tried forcing it. I've tried faking it until I would just magically suddenly fit in. I've spent ages just ignoring it, because if I bite my lip and bottle it up long enough it just goes away."

"I think you're worn out from trying to hold it in too long, and I want to make sure you're safe while you're dealing with things." She went over coping mechanisms, most of which I could have pulled up from a simple online search, and had, often. I'd been depressed, and anxious for years, I had just never known what this deep sort of disconnect was. And now I had a new word for it. "It sounds a lot like what you are experiencing is gender dysphoria. That's what not only your words, but your aura indicate."

"You were reading me?" I sat upright and glared. I thought that was private, and that she would wait for me to volunteer things, not just pry them out of me.

"I read everyone, especially if I am concerned they're a danger to themselves. It lets me know when we might be discussing things that are too sensitive or upsetting, and it lets me empathize better. I'm not a witch, I don't see your problems, I feel them." She touched her chest gently.

I squinted and tried to guess what she was, looking for any physical tells. Her ears, her eye color, anything that would clue me in.

"And now you're reading me." She chuckled, "But not mentally. You're trying to guess what I am. And if my guesses are right, you're going to really start hating when people do it to you."

What could she be mean by that? No one likes being read, it's just an annoyance of dealing with witches. And I didn't care if people looked at me anyway.

"So you're saying I have dysmorphia?"

"Dysphoria, and I'm saying it seems very possible. I'm not going to make a diagnosis right now. I want to talk with you more about this and find out more about these feelings you've been having. It can be a source of a lot of strife and anxiety, and the sooner I can confirm it or rule it out, the sooner I can better help you treat what has been bothering you so badly. And when that is figure out, many of the rest of your problems will be much easier to figure out, and I'll help you be better equipped to handle them."

I looked at her, disbelieving. It could not be this simple. And that stupid need of mine could not be the root of my problems.

"Are you saying the fact I might feel like I should be a guy is why I threw someone and destroyed some lockers?"

"In a way. I'm saying that the things that have been bothering you lately might be related to your outbursts and your feelings of being lost."

"I thought I was here so that you could make me no longer dangerous and I could go back to my self-inflicted miserable, boring life."

"Abigail, life doesn't have to be miserable. You don't have to suffer just because you're different, and it's my job to help you get better and help you figure out what you need to do to continue to be well."

"So you're not going to help me with my suspension?"

"I think you were protecting your friend and learned at the worst possible time that magical abilities like to pop up when they really, really shouldn't. It was dramatic, but no worse than if you'd hit him, and I'd say that it would have been deserved."

"You're not supposed to say that, you're an authority figure." I shot back, smug.

"Honestly fosters a sense of trust, and I need you to trust me if I'm going to help you."

She had a point, and had me cornered from a logical standpoint. I fell back in the chair dramatically, and threw an arm over the back of it, sitting sideways. "I don't want to be a transsexual."

"And you may not be. There's a chance this really is just all a phase. I'd like to give you someone safe to talk to. She's one of my clients and runs a little support group, and she's always happy to lend a hand and some guidance." She got up and went fishing in her purse for a business card, writing on the back. She peered over her glasses at me, "And Abigail, stay off the internet for now. I can recommend you a few resources I can verify, but I want you to figure this out on your own with a little input from people I trust. I don't want you self-diagnosing yourself with everything or getting worked into a panic because you are or aren't something." I hadn't heard her that firm before, and it startled me for seeming so benign. "I want you to raise any questions or concerns with me, and not just pull input from the anonymous masses. It can lead to problems."

"Do you get that a lot?"

"You have absolutely no idea how many self-diagnosed people I have heard of that claim to have multiple personalities or fictional characters living in their head, when they are in fact just budding writers who have yet to find a healthy outlet"

"That's, weird."

"Try fixing it."

"You're not supposed to say things like that." I laughed.

"I told you, I'm honest." She handed me a card with a number on it. Lilly Harrigan was the name, in fancy script.

I eyed it carefully.

"I promise, she's very nice, and she's very helpful without putting words in your mouth. I think you two will get along famously." She checked her watch again, "It looks like our time is up. I have a few more resources for you and some more homework. I'll put these in an envelope so your parents won't be as inclined to look through them."

"You're not telling my mom everything?"

"No, no, not at all. I respect the privacy of all of my clients, and I have no need to tell them anything unless I am concerned you are a danger to yourself or others."

"You don't think I'm dangerous?"

"Not at all." She smiled, not like a cat, but with radiating warmth. I took the card, and the envelope, and went back out to meet my mother.

On the way home, I pulled out my phone, and hesitantly texted the other number. I wasn't sure I had the nerve to call her; I had no idea who this person even was.

**[Hello Lilly. My shrink said I should get in touch with you on gender stuff.}**

I jumped when my phone sprang to life just a moment later.

**{Hiya! That sounds great want me to call? Or we can totes talk in person. Imma still a work and don't get off till late. Blah. -_-]**

**[Just text for now? Maybe we can meet later.}**

**{Okie Dokie! You sure you don't wanna chat today? I work at the *bux by the Hills.]**

I realized I really didn't speak girl, and it took me a while to decode what she was talking about. I knew what the hills were, it was the mall complex south-east of where I lived. Wait! I knew it! Starbucks!

**[I'll see what I can do. I don't have a car yet.}**

**{Awwwww :( Well say Hi if you can! My name's on my shirt. Here's a hint, I'm not the guy with the beard XD]**

**[Okay. Thank you!}**

**{TTFN Hon!]**

## Chapter Twenty

I walked the three blocks to the coffee shop on my own, keeping myself moving to stay warm. Will had left me at the mall, and we'd meet back up again by the carousel. Normally I wouldn't have minded, but right now it was only spring on a technicality. We'd gotten a dusting of snow the night before as one final middle finger from winter. I was thankful for the heat when I stepped inside, and my ears were stinging from the temperature change. A guy with a beard was behind the counter, as I knew that one wasn't Lilly. I filed in line, got a latte, and doused it in cinnamon.

I hadn't told my mom where I was; she'd never understand why I wanted to meet some strange girl my psychiatrist mentioned. It would probably be like meeting someone off the internet to her, which she also didn't know I had done before with a guy named Pierce who was looking for local fencers. He turned out to be another awkward sixteen year old. He also turned out to be in training for the Olympics, and it would have been impossible to explain meeting a guy online and coming home covered in bruises. We drifted apart because every single time, he kicked my ass.

I took a seat and pulled out my phone and big yellow brick. All I saw was the bearded guy and the occasional glance of a shaggy-haired boy that I was also pretty sure was not Lilly.

**[Here and waiting, Blue coat. Take your time.}**

I wanted to see if I could beat Metroid II in 45 minutes. Besides, I did catch her at work, I couldn't afford to be too picky. A girl came flouncing out in a long, tan skirt, and her green apron. "You must be Abby!" I looked over at her, then up, and froze.

It was her.

Blonde hair fell in loose curls around her cheeks, the rest pulled back into an artfully sloppy pony tail. Those hazel eyes met mine. It was her, without a doubt. Without the work wear and the horn-rimmed glasses, it was the girl from the islands, the girl with the weeping cherry tree.

"L-Lilly?" I tripped backwards over my own words.

"Doctor Calhoun gave me a call and warned me all about you." She chuckled, and sat in front of me. She had a natural, fluid grace to her that utterly offset the slightly large hands, long chin, and low alto. I would have never known she was anything if I wasn't looking for it. I suddenly felt bad for doing so, and I was starting to realize what my shrink had meant about reading. Her words set in, and I was almost worried.

"Warned you, huh?"

"All good things, don't worry. She said you were… questioning."

I gulped, and paused my game. "Is that okay?"

"Of course, hon. It's even one of the Qs."

"Qs?"

"In L.G.B.T.Q.Q.U.I.A. And well, a lot more letters. Sometimes we shorten it down to QUILTBAG."

"Quiltbag?"

"Queer, Undecided, Intersexed, Lesbian, Transgender, Bisexual, Asexual or allies, and Gay."

"That's…a mouthful." And I cringed at my own words. That could not have been the right thing to say by a long shot.

"Yeah, but you get used to it. Sometimes there are even more letters, but usually it's just LGBT, sometimes LGBTQ." She giggled, and flicked a strand of hair from her cheek. "It kind of becomes alphabet soup, doesn't it?"

"I guess." I blushed. "But yeah, I'm definitely a great big "Q" I guess"

"We're all been Q's sometime hon, it's nothing to worry about."

"Are you sure?"

"Definitely. Some people are late bloomers, too."

"Late bloomers?"

"They don't figure it out until they're much older. Some ladies who attend our meetings are around my mom's age."

"Oh, um, do any guys show up?"

"Oh! Oh, you're on that side of the fence. Sorry honey, I thought you were just super pretty already."

I bit my lip and shrunk, flustered by that. I didn't feel any semblance of pretty. Did she really think I was a boy trying to be a girl? I wasn't sure if I was flattered or offended.

"But yeah, some guys show up. Either way, you can ask some questions and see what you might be in for."

"In for?"

"If you decide to transition."

"But, I thought you'd tell me about treatment."

"Transitioning is treatment."

"You don't get it, I want to be cured!" I didn't realize how loud my voice had gotten once the blender in the background turned off.

Lilly nodded slowly. "I see, so you're still in that stage. Honey, er, Abby. This is the cure." She gestured gently to herself. "This is how treatment goes, and it made life so much better for me. It was what I needed."

"I don't think I need that." I shrunk, thankful for the shop being almost empty. I couldn't just turn into a boy, what would my parents think? What would Will think? I wanted to be happy as a girl, I wanted these feelings to all leave me in peace.

"Well, I'm here to talk. Dr. Cal said you might need an ear, 'cause you were really distressed by some things."

"Cal?"

"Calhoun, silly."

"Is there no such thing as doctor-patient confidentiality?" I rubbed at my temples. I was frustrated, and I felt vulnerable. This was awkward and it was just getting worse, "Look, I just want to be a normal girl, and I feel like my brain just won't let me do it, you know? Like something is broken."

"Hon, she wanted to help you. And you're not broken, you just might be different. I'm here to answer questions; I want to help you find the right path, even if that path is as a girl. I mean, there are lots of different ways to be a girl, you don't have to be a perfect one, you can be whatever kind you want to be."

"I'm sure there were lots of ways to be a boy, too, but you didn't do that did you?" I regretted it instantly. She winched.

Her eyes softened and she looked down, chewing on her knuckle. "Yes, yes there are a lot of ways, hon, but I wasn't a boy. Even if I was born male. It wasn't what was right for me. I want to help you figure out if it's right for you." Her response was gentle, almost skittish. I expected her to lash out at me, I had attacked her, and all she did was respond with concern. I had used the same question on her that Dr. Calhoun had used on me, and I had actively denied. Just four hours ago, I swore I wasn't a girl, and now I was attacking this girl for not staying male.

"I'm so sorry. I just—" I looked up at her, and she looked back at me, seeming almost on the edge of tears. She took a deep breath to center herself, and I felt her aura go from hurt to calmed, concerned even.

"Apology accepted." She smiled, it was weak, but it was genuine, "I just want to help. I know it can be scary when you first figure it out. It clicked for me when I was sixteen, and I didn't start anything until a few years later." She took my hand.

I flinched, but she just held it between hers. She had long, slender fingers, adorned with silver rings and charms. I was shaking in her embrace.

"Whatever you are, hon, I want to help you find your way."

I flinched, and I pulled away. "I'm sorry. I just don't think this is for me. Thank you, though. Thanks." I stood, and I left. I didn't look back until I was on my way up the hill, back to the mall to meet will again. I couldn't go back now, even if I needed her help. I just didn't know what to do. I wasn't ready for this; I wasn't ready to have such a big field of options thrown in my face when I couldn't even pick my favorite kind of slush at the gas station. I texted Will to meet me, and I went to the carousel. I watched flocks of little boys and girls run around, in different ways. I watched them exist in their own worlds, with probably no doubt if they were if the right path, and I wished that Syl had never said a thing to me. I wanted to be a girl, and happy as one. I cursed this new option; it didn't feel like the way to happiness and freedom, it felt like a path into a pit. My stomach tied itself into knots, and I waited for Will, more confused and unsure of myself than I had been before.

My phone buzzed, and I waited to see some message of hope and concern, that I was doing the wrong thing, or betraying myself. Instead, I got one that made me curse out loud. A mother covered her son's ears and shot me a glare.

**{You forgot your Gameboy ^_^}**

And she was right back in my life.

# Chapter Twenty-One

"I want to stop seeing Dr. Calhoun." I couldn't shake what I had done to Lilly, and I couldn't handle my options right now.

"Why, Pumpkin?" my dad asked.

"I can't tell you."

"Is something going on?" His force raised a bit at something, and I realized what he must have suspected.

"No, nothing like that. I just can't really tell you…"

"Abby, I need a clearer reason than that. She's close and takes our insurance, and your mother says she's very highly recommended."

"I don't like her."

"Okay, why not?"

"I… still can't tell you." I wanted to be cured. I wanted to scream from the rooftops that I was a girl and I refused to be anything else and that my heart should be beaten severely and buried alive for implying anything else. I refused to add just another kind of freak to the list of words that already described myself.

"Pumpkin, I need a reason. I mean, if I need to get lawyers involved."

"Dad I don't need a lawyer, she's not doing anything like that." I wondered what I did to deserve this fate. Why couldn't I just have good old fashioned teenage anger issues? I would have killed for normal angst and boyfriend problems.

"Is it because she's asking tough questions and making you think about things?"

"Maybe." He had no idea how deep that little rabbit hole went, but I didn't want to be disowned.

"That's her job, Pumpkin. She's supposed to make you think about things so you can fix them. It's not comfortable when you let things heal, you know."

"But my brain's not itchy like a scab!" He gave me a look, and I realized that one made a lot more sense in my head. I was grateful that he let that one slide without comment.

"Abby, sometimes it's hard to face things and deal with them, but that's a big part of being grown up and dealing with your problems like an adult. You'll be one in a year, after all. Then this will all be a lot more serious."

"Yes Dad, I know. I'm not just being a child about this."

"Then I need you to prove that by continuing to go, even if you don't like it. I need you to show me that you can do this. If you have any real concerns, like she's not listening to you, or she's abusive with you in any way, then we need to know. But you can't just stop going because you don't like it."

"But I don't like what she said is wrong with me!"

"And what did she say?"

"I can't tell you." I cringed as he literally face palmed. I couldn't blame him; I had to look utterly obtuse from a outside observation. I wasn't just being some whiny teenager that didn't want to do something hard, I wanted to find someone to cure me. I would have given anything right now to just be normal. I would have taken assault charges, and have gladly been just another angry dumb kid, rather than have this hanging over my head.

"Pumpkin, I know you're a lot more grown up than you act at times, and I really need you to do this. Not just for your mom and I or for the school, but you should do this for yourself, okay?"

I nodded, and felt like my brain was going to spill out if I did so too vigorously. My hands were tied, and my mind was running in anxious circles around the rest of me as I tried to catch up. Why did Syl have to be right?

No. She wasn't. She had to be wrong. I'd give anything to make her wrong. I raided my closet, and pulled out a dusty, lint-covered skirt. It was in there from when we all attended Mass, which was less and less frequent with my mom's work hours. I looked in the mirror and cringed at the sight of my own hairy legs. They had never bothered me before, it wasn't like I wore shorts. If the skirt could talk, it would be screaming in protest at being wrapped around those legs. I rummaged for tights in my sock drawer, and found none. I couldn't recall seeing any since I was fourteen, and I think I borrowed my mother's then. I rummaged in the closet, throwing cargo pants onto a pile of their own kind. Blue jeans hid here and there, and I finally found it, a long, black, broomstick skirt. It had been one of my mother's, a parental hand-me down. I loved it on her, it made her look like a real witch, and she gave it to me after she had Laurie and it didn't quite fit. It barely fit me, I was all hips, but it hid my legs.

I found the closest thing I could to a girl's shirt. It wasn't an easy task in my wardrobe. It was technically just another graphic T-shirt, but this one wasn't gaming or heavy metal focused. Well, technically it was an internet browser joke, but mostly it was a cute fox. I shifted to the only real bra I owned, from a wedding where I was a bridesmaid with a sleeveless dress.

I looked in the mirror, and I didn't see myself. I was going to make myself see otherwise, I had to. I had heard for years to fake it till I made it, and I was going to do just that. I had no choice. There was nowhere else to go from here, and neither Lilly nor Dr. Calhoun were going to fix me in the way I needed to be fixed.

I looked utterly ridiculous. I didn't feel gorgeous, or pretty, or even feminine. I felt awkward, and my legs were much too breezy for my liking. I felt like I was in drag.

My phone, ever the harbinger of bad news, buzzed merrily at me. It was a sadistic little jerk.

**{I still have your game boy. It is safe with me ^_^ I can drop it off, or you can go get it.]**

**{Playing Pokemon Red again, Yay!]**

How could she still be so cheerful and nice to me after what I did to her? She could send me my Gameboy's ransom note right now, or send me pictures of her smashing it to pieces. She could have even just said that it was hers now. Instead, she was just using my batteries up. How terrible.

**[I have to come rescue it, don't I?}**

**{Yep yep! Or I can come get you and we can chat a lil bit]**

**[Do I have any other options?}**

**{Nope.]**

**[Can't you give it to Dr. Calhoun? I see her Friday.}**

**{I don't see her for a month ^_^]**

I sat on the bed, and thought, hard. I could go get it back, but I'd have to talk to her again.

**[Maybe tomorrow, my ride goes back to school.}**

**{I can come get u 2nite.]**

**[No thanks, Lilly.}**

**{I'm making Creeeepes.]**

**[No thanks, Lilly.}**

**{With bacooooon]**

**[You're cruel.}**

**{Crepes of friendship? :3]**

**[I'm a girl, I don't need your help.}**

**{I'm friends with girls and boys!]**

I stared at the screen, and it shone back at me. I didn't know what to make of this, at all. She still wanted to be my friend. I had been a complete ass to her, and she wanted to see me. Her cheer was infectious, even if she was trying too hard.

**{Trans* or not, you seem nice, and scared too.]**

**I resisted the urge to correct her grammar. Will was rubbing off on me.**

**{I wanna help!!!]**

**[Come get me, maybe?}**

**{Eeeeeeeeeeeeeeeeeeeeeeeeeeeeee!]**

The girl at the cherry tree wasn't going to let me fall again.

## Chapter Twenty-Two

She pulled up to the corner of my street, and the next nearest. I shivered under my bulky coat; it did nothing for the cold wind gnawing at my legs. I was beginning to see why skirts were a terrible idea, especially in winter. Gender-nonsense aside, it was all seeming extremely impractical, and without gender nonsense aside, I felt grossly uncovered.

The car that pulled up was primer grey, devoid of badging, and from the sound of it, lacking a muffler. As if making up for the lackluster exterior, the inside was festive. It contained no less than two dream catchers and a whole herd of My Little Pony toys grazing on the dash, and the bright floral and black seat covers that you find at every auto parts store. She leaned over and popped open my door, grinning up at me like the Cheshire Cat.

I held my ground. "Gameboy?"

"After crepes."

"You could be an ax murderer."

"Would an ax murderer make bacon crepes?"

"Possibly." I didn't see most ax murderers as being the kind of person to fill their car with plastic ponies, though. Maybe it was to lure me into a false sense of security.

She looked over her glasses at me, and summoned her best doe eyes. "Are you sure?" She started to rummage in her purse.

I sighed, "Promise you aren't an ax murderer?"

"Pinkie swear!" She held up a pink horse and grinned broadly. It was the kind of unrestrained grin that would have felt fake from almost every person I had met, but something about her made it seem genuine. Maybe it was the fact she was almost vibrating with glee as she did it.

"Okay. For crepes." I sat down on one of the blindingly fuchsia seat covers. It was fuzzy. I buckled up, and we zoomed off. I found myself bracing, as she flicked her way through the gears before we were even out of the neighborhood. I watched Rockville pass by, and we went south.

"So, are you a witch too?" she asked me, as we shot down a country road, car rattling and vibrating away.

"Yeah, It's why I'm seeing Mrs, er, Dr. Calhoun."

"Late bloomer?"

"No, threw somebody and got suspended."

"Oh dear. That's terrible," she squeaked, and I wondered if she was being sarcastic.

"Well, it's two weeks off anyway."

"At least you weren't expelled. Why did you do that?"

I leaned on the door, and the overhead light popped on for a moment. I sulked upright instead. "I didn't mean to, it was an accident." I couldn't escape being under inquisition, could I? I sprawled in my seat, and leaned with a bit more care on the door.

"Oh, sudden new powers? I know how that goes, I just started being able to dream walk one day. Right into my roommate's. Ew." She giggled.

"Wait, you live on your own?"

"Yeah. Have for almost two years now."

"How old are you?" My ax murderer sense was tingling.

"Just eighteen, why so?"

"And you live alone?"

"It's a long story. And I don't live alone, I have roommates. So technically, I live independently. I divorced my parents and everything."

"I see." I had no idea if she was being sarcastic or joking, or maybe even serious, and I wasn't sure if I should ask. I settled for my default, an awkward laugh followed by clamming up. It wasn't a perfect strategy, but it would do. I watched the countryside go by, and the last trace of my home down as we slipped under the highway bridge. I picked up a pony and examined it; it was a unicorn, a grey one. "Wait, you have magic? But boys can't have magic." My voice became a frightened squeak as my sentence tapered off, too late to fix my mistake.

"Well, I'm not a boy anymore, now am I? Actually, it kind of freaked me out at the time, to be honest. I was on hormones for six months, and then suddenly things started to get all witchy. I'm from the right lines, got it on both sides of the family, and it just kicked in one day. I still can't fly or anything…" Her voice softened, and I felt the sweeping pull of longing in it. "But I'm super giddy for what I have, I mean, dream walking is fantastic when you find a good one to go hang out in. I usually do it when I meditate before work in the morning."

"Yeah, I know."

"You do?" She glanced over at me a moment, her perky squeak had dropped out of her voice. I was startled by a low alto, and an equally confused one at that.

"Nevermind." I looked down at myself, all sprawled legs, and clicked my knees together. I could hear my mother's voice in my head from the last time I wore this skirt, reprimanding me for not sitting like a lady. The silence drew itself out, and I sat with my hands in my lap. I'd been hogging the arm rests too.

She suddenly sat up right, and looked directly at me, "Aaron? Are you…?"

I nodded, and shrunk. I looked forward. Then I screamed.

"Car!"

I was thrown into the door, and the overhead light went off again on impact. The tires screeched and the suspension crackled as she dodged the headlights that had just threatened to pounce. We crossed the white line on the wrong side of the road and veered into the shoulder. The engine bogged and stalled.

"Oh god I'm so sorry. I never do, I mean, Are you…? Oh god I'm sorry, are you okay Aaron?" She clung to the wheel, color drained from her face and knuckles.

I tried to pull myself together, "I'm all right." My voice was an octave higher, and I realized I was almost crying. Some boy I was.

"I can't believe it…" She trailed off, and started the car again. We were silent the last mile to her place. I wasn't angry, just startled, and my heart threatened to pound its way out of a vein in my neck. It wasn't an apartment; it was a little colonial house with hibernating rose bushes out front. It was far from the shady complex I had been picturing, it was quaint, and would have been post card worthy with a soft dusting of snow and a few strategically placed chickadees. Perhaps with a grazing deer or two, or some round little cottontail rabbits, you know, cute New England stuff. There were two more cars in the little gravel lot, and she pulled in between them. "Are you sure you're okay?" She touched my hand. I flinched, and my skin bristled. She was soft, and I was as prickly as ever.

"Yeah, I'm fine." I zipped up my coat before opening the door. My legs were cold, but my chest was properly hidden. The dark feeling inched in, and Lilly took my arm gently.

She smiled. "I know that feeling. Come on, we'll have crepes, and talk."

"You can sense, too?"

"Nope, you just looked terrified and confused. I know that look. I used to see it every day in the mirror."

I resisted her pulling and became stone on her walkway, "I don't want to be transgender." I tried to be firm, and it fell apart. My voice shattered into desperation, "I just want to be normal."

"Then I have a question." She took my wrists, and looked me in the eye. The night was quiet and still around us, bitter cold aside from the warmth of her hand. Her eyes flickered under the porch light, lively and intense, but more severe than I had ever seen her. I braced for something harsh, for her to finally snap back at me.

"I want you to think about this, hard. You don't have to answer for me, but you need to answer yourself. Is it that you don't want to be 'A transsexual' or that you don't want to be male?" I wished that she would have said something cruel, and not something more painful, as she inflicted the sting of honesty. "Because these are two very different things. I'm not someone who's going to be forever between genders, I am a girl, I'm going to continue to become even more of one. Being female is what makes me feel whole, and the goal I'm chasing not the idea of just changing my gender on a lark. So, think, Aaron, Abigail, either, what do you want to be?"

She looked me dead in the eye, and I wanted to disappear. I felt small, and ashamed, as I stood here in my best attempt at being that which I felt nothing for. The strange feeling was brewing. The night grew darker, the storm brewing around me. I was all too aware of everything that was wrong with me, and I waited for it to swallow me alive. I winced and waited for it to take me away. Instead, something on the outside, something real, embraced me. I opened my eyes, as loose strands of golden hair brushed my cheeks. My chin pressed into her soft, suede jacket, my head was tucked almost under her chin, as her thin arms held me with more strength than I would have ever expected.

"I know how you feel right now. You're not in your own head, or your own body. You're feeling a divide that just gets bigger and bigger as you get older, and you don't know where you're going yet, because you still don't know what you are." She exhaled slowly, a soft plume of steam. "I know what it looks like, that dark shadow that makes the world so much darker, and feels like it's pulling you out of your real body.

"The dreams don't lie, and I've talked to you for a very long time now. Don't you remember?"

I shook my head numbly, and something small and bright slipped into the view of my mind's eye. "You caught me."

"I'm kind of a butterfingers..." She blushed. Her cheek was almost against mine. "I didn't mean to let go."

"I've dreamed about you a lot."

"I know, I've been there. I always wait at your tree for you."

"I thought it was your tree."

She shook her head, "You made that world, not me. I thought it was one of the most beautiful dreams I had been in."

Clearly she wasn't used to spending most of it falling to her death. I didn't get to take in the scenery in quite the same manner when it flew past me at sixty miles per second. "I hate it; I always wake up feeling terrible. I don't usually remember my dreams anyway, I don't know what makes those ones so special. Aside from, you know, the whole suddenly a boy thing."

"That's a pity, because you make beautiful worlds, at least all of the ones I've been into. And you make a pretty good boy, I wasn't suspecting a thing when I talked to you."

"Really? Wait, have you been following me a while?"

"Ever since I saw you fall."

My aura of sarcasm fell apart again. My shell had been cracked, and I clung close to her for something solid to anchor myself upon, "Thank you." I could recall so little of our time together, but I was so grateful to have someone who knew where I had been. Someone had tried to save me, even if it was from myself.

"So, Abby or Aaron?"

"Do I have to be sure right now?"

"Nope!" She was back to being infectiously cheerful and bounced on her heels in the cold spring air.

I pulled back, and nodded. "Then Aaron, just for tonight."

"Okay then!" She hugged me again, and looked me up and down. Mischief flooded her eyes and her smile broke into a huge grin. "Nice skirt, Aaron."

## Chapter Twenty-Three

I loitered in her kitchen, and watched the crepe process unfold. It was every bit as quaint on the inside as it was on the outside, if a little out-dated. The wall-paper was the kind of green floral I saw at my grandmother's house, and the kitchen had a running chicken theme, from the soap dispenser to the salt shakers, with a barnyard scene painted on the decorative interior shutters.

"So…you like…chickens?" I picked up the pepper hen, grasping for something to talk about.

"Not really, actually. I like matching, and the place came almost completely furnished. So, the chicken theme stayed. I'm the only one in the kitchen anyway, so I'm the one who has to put up with it." The whole place had a very grandmotherly feel, cozy, warm, and frighteningly clean. It was hard to picture three college students living here, without so much as a shoe on the floor or a couch pillow out of line. This was a fanatical level of clean I only saw in showrooms and people over sixty. The only hint of a modern touch in the room was a large, flat-screen television that was mounted over an old wooden cabinet stand. I could easily picture a doily or curtain thrown over it.

"So your roommates don't cook?" I wandered back on topic.

"Nah, it's all pizza and carry out, and the occasional tacos. If they do anything, they use the microwave." I hadn't even noticed it, an old metal behemoth with a dial, not buttons. It didn't even register as a microwave at a glance.

"You get premium channels on that thing?" I chuckled weakly at my own comment.

"Just Russian radio stations. It came with the kitchen, too. I think it's almost an antique." She flipped a crepe, and plated it after what seemed like just a few seconds, then poured in the batter for another. I watched it dance in mind-air as she tossed it as well, and caught the golden round in the pan.

"That's amazing."

"Not much of a cook?" She added that one to the pile. "Can you slice these?" She slid a carton of mushrooms across the gold-flecked countertop.

"At least they aren't onions."

"Oh, you can do those too!"

I grumbled quietly under my breath, I hated cutting onions. I did the mushrooms in a huff, and put on my best poker face for the little yellow onion.

"It's okay for boys to cry, though know." She giggled.

"I'm not..." I inhaled the onion fumes and sputtered, my sinuses and eyes were suddenly ablaze, "a boy yet."

"But you identify as one, yes?"

"I guess so…" Tears began running own my cheeks. I tried to blink them away. "Done!" I shoved the cutting board in her direction and washed my hands in the sink.

"Try the soap, it's coffee scented and works great on onion stink." Soon the air was filled with the smell of bacon, which arose victorious over the noxious onion cloud. I scrubbed my hands until they stung, but the odor still clung to them. Lilly started to assemble our dinner, and I hovered nearby. There wasn't a dining room, or a table for one, and she handed me the plate. I stood and stared dumbly at her, then followed into her bedroom.

"Have a seat wherever." She artfully flopped into the biggest bean bag I had ever seen. I looked around for a chair, with only a drawing desk and a computer as my options, and favored the computer. It hummed softly to itself and green lights flickered off and on along the case. It didn't look like a girl's room, or a boy's room, it was a geek's room. The walls were blue, and lined with posters from 80s fantasy films. I turned and was uncomfortably close to an almost life-size one of the goblin king. "Dig in!"

The savory glory that was the taste of bacon exploded across my taste buds, and any bitterness I had harbored over the onions was gone. "Never had crepes before," I said with a full mouth. I liked anything with bacon, even flimsy little pancakes.

"Toss me a root beer!" She pointed to the mini-fridge nearby, and I passed it off to her, and grabbed one myself. We talked, everything from Jim Henson to Doctor Who, to Connecticut weather and the second-winter that was due to hit. "I hate driving in the snow." She hunkered down in her beanbag, setting her plate aside.

"Then might I suggest Maryland? Or Georgia, no snow there." I'd never lived anywhere but here, and I couldn't imagine a winter without a foot of snow here and there.

"No, it's worth it. I moved here, and I'm going to stay here, even if it means the snow."

"You moved to Connecticut, and you don't like snow?"

"It was safer for me. Besides, I'm not from that much farther south, just Pennsylvania."

"Safer than cows and fields and mountains?"

She nodded and sighed, "I had to get away from my family, and Pennsylvania has really crappy gender discrimination laws. I could have been fired or kicked out of an apartment over it. So I drove my trusty lemon all the way out here to stay with some friends and I've been here ever since."

"Your parents didn't take it well, huh?"

She sighed and threw her hands up in the air, "That's the understatement of the century. I told you, I divorced them."

"Seriously?" I leaned forward in my seat, eyes wide.

"They threw me out and everything, wanted to send me off to some program, wanted to sue my psychiatrist for malpractice over the diagnosis. I lived with my aunt for a little while, took my GED test, and bailed. It wasn't a choice I made lightly." She smiled weakly at me, "My mom calls me sometimes these days, I think it just takes time…"

"What about your dad?"

She went quiet, and stared at the ceiling. "The last thing he said to me is that he wasn't going to raise a faggot son in his house."

I cringed with no idea how to respond.

"My mom signs his name on cards, so I don't know what's going on now. At least they've started calling me Lilly."

"What was your name?"

She laughed, "That's kind of rude, you know. But since you're a friend, and you don't know any better… it was Drake." Her expression fell flat, like she'd found a fly in her crepes.

"You make a better Lilly."

Her expression shot right back up. "I think so, too. You're lucky, you can get things started in this state, and if your parents panic, you can crash here if you want."

I cringed, not finding that comforting. I wasn't even sure of things myself, I wasn't sure how I could break it to them, or if I even could at all. They had put up with so much of me already, and they genuinely loved me, I couldn't imagine them just turning on me like that. I couldn't fathom my docile father telling me to leave and never come back, or my mother wanting me out of her life. It had never occurred to me that I could choose to do something that would make my parents push me out of their lives. I shrunk, and hugged my knee, forgetting about my skirt entirely.

"I bet it won't go too badly, though. I mean, you can ask Dr. Cal to help handle things, she can be a great mediator."

I nodded numbly, her words just barely resonated as horrible scenarios invaded my thoughts, "Yeah, yeah that could work." And I was back to wondering how hard it could be to stay female forever. I wasn't sure if being happier was worth risking everything. What would my parents think? What would Will think? My train of thought derailed, as I realized this could lose me the only close friend I had, the friend who was almost more to me than family. We'd never really mentioned this kind of thing, what would he say? The whole dynamic could change in one swoop, and I could lose everything I treasured about our relationship. The last word rang in my head, and I quickly corrected it to friendship. We were friends, just friends, and now we would always be just friends, assuming he still wanted to talk to me. Transition suddenly seemed to solve fewer and fewer of my problems, as where it opened one door, it closed two more.

"It's not usually as bad as my family was." Lilly seemed to know exactly what was going through my head, "Especially if they're from around here, people are a lot more tolerant. Besides, you don't have to come out now, you should think about it a lot longer, get to know yourself."

"If you say so." My head wasn't in the conversation now. I don't know how long passed before she suggested something that made my heart sink.

"I should take you back home. It's getting late."

They didn't know anything, and I was already afraid to face my parents. I kept failing them as a daughter, and I wasn't sure if they would welcome another son. This evening's revelation hadn't solved any of my problems.

## Chapter Twenty-Four

For two days in a row, I didn't get out of bed when I heard Will out tinkering in the morning, and I didn't bother moving until I heard the bus come back in the afternoon. I had wallowed through breakfast, and skipped lunch, and my mother had no idea I hadn't even moved. I picked at dinner, as a family, and retreated back into my bedroom. My mind would not leave me be, as I tossed and turned, floating in and out of sleep. I wasn't Abby anymore, not in my dreams, and not awake. I had a name for this feeling, and it somehow made it so much worse. I missed waiting to bloom, waiting for the day when I suddenly became the girl I had been waiting to be, and everything would click and fall together. I was waiting for the day when this would all, suddenly, work. Now I knew the way out. There wasn't any waiting for that day anymore. I had to reach out and seize it. I was terrified. I couldn't just sit back and wait for my life to get better.

I was doomed. No, worse, I was fucked.

There was a knock at my door, which pulled me from my half-asleep daze. "Yes, Mom?"

"It's me."

I sat up sharply, "Will?" I pulled the blankets up sharply, and bundled them around my middle. The door opened. "How did you get in?"

"Your dad never locks the garage, remember?" He seemed nervous and looked down at the floor, "I haven't seen you in a few days, and well, um…did I screw something up?"

"No, it's a long story, haven't really been feeling well."

"That sounds like a short story."

"I guess it wasn't long after all." I forced a chuckle.

"You sure you're not mad?" His eyebrows arched together and he sighed.

"Yeah, I'm sure. It's just…stuff. Um, can I get dressed?"

"Don't mind me." He grinned mischievously.

"Yeah, out." I threw a pillow at him when he didn't budge instantly. I dressed in a hurry, back in my cargo pants and obscure metal shirt. I felt like myself again, well, almost like myself. I felt like Abby two months ago, and not the Aaron I was sure I was now "Safe."

"I could have just turned around. Not like you haven't seen me more than once."

"I'm not a pervert."

"Neither am I." That was lame, at least coming from Will. His ability to fight back wasn't quite what it usually was. He was either losing his touch, or something was up.

I stretched, and sat back on the bed. "I can go back in five days."

"Trust me, you don't want to." He leaned in the doorway and held his own biceps, staring at his feet.

"It can't be that bad. I mean, can it?"

"They're out for blood, Abby. Everyone knows what we are now, and we can't just hide in the back of the room and pretend to be normal anymore."

"Wait, seriously? But your brother was fine."

"Yeah, well neither of us are Brian! We're already social fuckups, Abby, we can't just suddenly be seen as magical and mysterious. You're a loose cannon, and I'm an Easter pet, and things aren't just going to go back to how it was!" He gestured sharply and winced, cupping his shoulder and rolling it.

"What did they do to you?"

"It was just shove and a bad landing. I've spent three days with everyone trying to make me transform. I've been poked, kicked, shoved, and startled all because someone wants to see if it's even real. I used to just be able to sit and read a book and not have ass-hats throwing carrots at me!" He held his arm still; Will nearly couldn't talk without gesturing and waving his hands around.

"They threw carrots at you? That's middle school bullsh-"

"Abs I swear, carrots. It's junior high all over again, and I'm the wounded gazelle." His analogy kind of fell apart, but I knew this wasn't really the right time to correct him. He spotted my confusion and threw his hands up, "Oh you know what I meant." He flinched back again, and let his arm hang limp at his side, other crossed over his chest. Will glared at his own shoes. His eyes were boring through the carpet. Rigidly curled, his posture was a mixture of defiant and vulnerable, nearly wrapped around himself. The anxiety flooded into me as well, I could never stop reading him. I felt my heart pick up, and I bit my cheek to reel my focus back in. I wasn't going to panic about this when he needed my help more.

"I'm so sorry, Will." I took his hand, and he flinched, eyeing me carefully. The hairs on his arm bristled, and his pulse shot up, I could feel it in his fingers. "I shouldn't have done anything… I should have kept my cool."

"Don't hog all the credit; you didn't turn into a bunny. I'd be fucked either way and probably with some broken ribs to show for it." He looked down at my hand, our hands. He didn't pull away. His eye narrowed, almost like he was examining me, and I felt an aura of deep confusion. I pulled back, and stuffed my hands in my pocket. He exhaled, and pulled me into a hug. It could have been nice, and I appreciated the sentiment, but less appreciated hitting my chin and nose into his collarbones, and his ribs all jabbed back at once.

"Ow." I shifted to protect my nose again.

"Shut up. Hugging." He grumbled into my ear. He rested his chin on my head, and sighed. "I don't know what to do now."

"Home school?" I suggested half-sarcastically.

"That's what my mom keeps saying. That or ship me off to some private school to the east." There were an assortment of places past the ridge with names like St. so and so's academy. They were expensive, and a bit antiquated, if pretty to drive past. "Or I can go to the local Catholic school."

"You're not Catholic."

"Yeah, I know.

"The uniform would be dapper and adorable." I smirked.

"I think I'd look quite classy, thank you." He pulled back and stared down at me.

"That's true, you already dress like you're wearing a uniform, Mr. doesn't own a T-shirt."

"Riiight, and I'm supposed to take fashion advice from camo pants and bands with umlauts." He poked me in the chest.

"Hey, they're actually Norwegian, not posers or anything." I broke the hug and crossed my arms, glaring right back at him. My desire to look indignant overruled the fact that I hated touching my own chest.

"Metal hipster." He snorted.

"Dandy boy." I shot back. A bit of an antique, but fitting, "You're such a fop, Will."

"I like looking respectable, unlike some people I know, or are we bringing grunge back?"

We were fighting, but this kind of good-natured bickering was what the last ten years of friendship was built on. A few good-natured insults always seemed more natural to me than how my interaction had gone with other girls. Even as a witch, they were hard to read, and I could never tell what was an actual compliment and what was an insult. I watched them form and shatter circles all the time at school, and I realized I only really wanted one anchor in the world.

"Come flying with me?"

His eyebrows raised, and he tilted his head, I could tell he was baffled without needing to read him. "You broke your broom. Don't you ever only get one and bond to it or something?"

I face palmed lightly. "I can fly with any broom, so long as it's light enough. It's just not as special. There's one in the garage I used to play with." It was from back when I didn't have mine yet, and wanted to race around the yard, back when flying was still something that interested me.

"I'll warm up the bike, you get your stuff." He had a spring in his step as he left, he seemed almost cheerful again. I had been so wrapped up in myself these past few days, I'd forgotten to look after my friends. I heard the world's fastest weed whacker fire up, and I grabbed my helmet and broom. I was determined to make a good day out of this, somehow.

# Chapter Twenty-Five

It wasn't any easier this time around to get the broom going. It pitched to the side at the slightest lean, and seemed determined to throw me off. I was riding a pine bronco thirty feet above the ground, and my only spectator had laughed himself asthmatic. The broom spiraled down suddenly, and I clung, trying to stay on, and leaned back to pull it out of its tailspin. Will dodged as I plowed over the spot he'd been on. The bristles brushed the ground, and the grass nicked my knuckles. I pulled up, and it shot into the sky, somehow, I was still on it. Thirty feet. Forty. Sixty. I stopped guessing and shut my eyes tight, holding on for dear life, gently leaning forward to balance it out and not go plowing into the dirt.

It leveled itself and I swooped gently to the left, letting the broom bank softly. The wind blew back my hair, and I watched the farm below drift, a gently rolling scene below. It was too perfect to last, I tried to curve it the other way, and I was suddenly chasing my own tail, then dropping like a stone. It had a mind of its own, a channel for my anxieties, which seemed bent on physically ruining my life at this point. I pulled back on it and let my weight go towards the tail, and it leveled, zipping along like it had meant to do that and was certainly not planning on sending me falling to my death in some farmer's field. It shot along, quick yet passive, and I was almost starting to trust it. I knew I had to trust myself, and calm my own mind down, but it was so much easier to channel my thoughts into the object under me. I gave it a personality and called it a lot of words I'm normally too polite to shout, but it was slowly calming down. The broom rolled lazily to the left, banking softly without flipping me upside down or corkscrewing into the dirt. It was almost trustworthy.

I exhaled slowly, and sent it into a leisurely spiral, trying to recall my mother's lessons about treating it as an extension of your body, a part of yourself. Given my recent revelation this felt a little Freudian. I chuckled immaturely at the idea of just how it could be the, ahem, extension of my psyche.

The broom must not have had a sense of humor. It didn't appreciate my inner monologue of phallic giggling, and I went nose-diving into the ground. It buried itself nose-first in the dirt and stuck firm. It bucked under me, and I went rolling off of it. I lay on the ground, and wondered if I was actually hurt or if it was just my dignity, and realized it was only a rock under my shoulder. I thrust a hand into the air, and gave a very feeble thumbs up.

"Walk it off!" called Will, "I want to ride it with you later!"

"Thank you for your concern, I think I only broke two ribs and lost an eye!" I yelled back.

"Only a flesh wound!" That bastard.

I sat up, and the world rolled a bit, I'd almost forgotten what it was like to be still. I pulled it from the dirt, and mounted up again, my shoes and pants were caked in mud.

"Oh come on. Up." I tried to get a running start and launch again, but it didn't seem to be in the mood anymore. I must have offended it.

"Aw, is it over?" Will asked, having shuffled over, obviously terribly concerned for my well being or missing the chance for a ride.

"I think I pissed it off, and it decided it was done with me." I took another waddling start, running like a duck and jumping into the air. I landed square on my knees, and shouted a profanity. The birds in a nearby tree scattered. I had clearly offended their delicate sensibilities. Will offered me a hand up, and I took it, forcing my legs to straighten again, knees on fire. "Yeah, it's done, now it's just out for blood."

"It had its first taste and wants more. Into the wood chipper with thee!" He pointed at the broom, which lay limp on the ground. "Yep, it's definitely plotting our demise right now." He went back to his bike and put on his gear, more amused than I was as I stiffly hobbled after him.

"Jerk." I picked up the garage's broom. Even I wasn't quite sure who in present company I was insulting, but it worked for any of them. Will mounted the bike and fired it up. He was jealous of my ability to fly, and I was jealous of his. His own mount was no less fantastic than mine, a gleaming series of semi-circles and chrome flourishes. I almost felt bad comparing it to a lawn mower, almost. He had his own way of flying, even if he didn't think so, but I'd never felt a sensation more like it. It rumbled beneath him, and I slid onto the seat, garage broom tucked under my arm and sticking out front like a lance. "Let's go back, it's getting cold." I yelled into his helmet where his ear should be. He nodded once, and I gave the signal for takeoff. The Vespa zoomed along, and I was warmed by the last rays of the sun, before the world went dark and quiet. The ground was a blur, and the wind ran its long, delicate fingers through my hair. Stars slipped out of hiding above us, one by one. It really was just like flying.

## Chapter Twenty-Six

"Where have you been? Shoes!" My father's concern had turned into horror the moment he had laid eyes on my mud caked boots. I shed them on the stairs into the garage and put them on the mat. My socks weren't much cleaner and had to go too. "Honestly, did he take that thing off-road?" He cringed as I held out my socks, taking them to the hamper. "Pants too!"

"Yes Dad." I stifled my amusement.

"It looks like you had… fun." He tried to hide the disdain in his voice. My father was two things: fastidious and open minded, and right now they were viciously at odds.

"Just the unimproved roads by The Snip." The road to the nearby lake was a favorite place for anything that could handle a little mud.

"Oh, well. I'm glad you enjoyed yourself. Have a seat." He winced at the sight of my shirt, the cleanest thing left, but scolding for filthy clothes was something he was used to doing with Laurie. He returned to his pot. Once I changed, I could smell that the air was filled with the aroma of meat and vinegar, and I was worried. This could not possibly end well.

"What's for dinner?" I asked, skeptical of the simmering pots and cast iron piled on our stove.

"It's a Polish dish."

"Like the sausage?" I asked, hopefully.

"Kind of. It has bacon in it." For once, that did not raise my hopes. "Why don't you make a cup of tea?" His voice wavered a bit. He knew I didn't like tea; it was just part of my calming ritual. Will liked tea. Something was up.

"Sure. Everything okay?"

He turned and looked back at me. "Not quite, Abby. Now, we're not mad, I want you to know that. We don't blame you, and your mother and I will get this sorted out as soon as we can."

This couldn't end well. He hadn't even told me the news yet, and I was bracing for impact, curled around my empty mug as I stared down the kettle and waited. He almost never called me by my first name, not when actually addressing me. It was usually pumpkin, or chickadee, or some assortment of other little pet quips he'd assigned to me. My mind reeled. Maybe my psychiatrist had called, and maybe those rules on doctor patient confidentiality didn't apply to minors. Could he know? There was no way he could have found out, unless, damn it, Sylvia! I swallowed my feelings back, from terror to rage. "So what is it?"

"Well, your school called." He started, and trailed off a moment, pulling himself back together after waving a wooden spoon in the air for a moment. This already could not be as bad as I was fearing. He exhaled and continued, "They don't want you to come back, Abby."

"Am I expelled?" I stared up at him, stunned.

"Not officially. It won't be an expulsion on your record or anything like that. They just don't think it will be a mutually safe learning environment for you or the other students."

"So they think either they're going to tear into me, or I'm going to start throwing people around like rag dolls? That's a load of shhhhhhhhhh…." I caught myself, and let the sound just taper off. He was still my dad. I was still not allowed to swear.

"I know. I know it's bad. Your mother and I are talking to someone else about this, so we can see what our options are. Maybe Grace, er, Mrs. Lagai was right about us possibly having a discrimination suit against them."

"I don't want to sue anyone, Dad, I just want to have my old life back, crappy school and all."

"I know, Pumpkin, but this could be very good for your future, there might be a silver lining, and it could help pay for you to further your education."

"I don't want to sue anyone, I just want life to go back to how it was. Why is that so fucking hard!" I slammed the cup down, throwing out the teabag and scattering sugar all over the countertop. I flinched, so did he. He breathed a long sigh and rubbed his forehead.

"Language, Abby." He sounded more exhausted than anything, and I was instantly embarrassed.

"Sorry, Dad.'

"I know, but we need to make the best of this, and we need to do it soon. I don't want you losing a whole year's credit over this. You're too smart to be held back a year because of all of this. Your mother and I need to talk and go over your options."

"Wait, does she know yet?" I sat up straighter in my chair.

"No, Honey, not yet." He rubbed his face again and exhaled slowly.

"Can I stay at Will's house this evening?" I tried to ask that as casually as possible, but I sounded only slightly less than terrified.

"She's not going to bite you. This isn't your fault."

"Yes Dad." It felt like my fault, a lot like my fault, and I was pretty sure that is how my mother was going to take it. I saw no easy way out of this. The meaning of everything he said was starting to sink in. I wasn't going to go back to that school anymore, or take the bus with Will again. No more sneaking a ride with Brian, or morning rides on the world's fastest, er, the Vespa. There would be no more early morning flying along the back roads with my best friend, or programming club meetings. I would be starting over, and I wouldn't have Will at my side through any of it, not unless we both went to Saint So and So's together.

The kettle boiled, and I filled my teacup. Wordlessly, I shuffled to my room, past the den of the sleeping witch, which I passed being extra quiet. She had no idea what had just happened, and I didn't want to be under the same roof when she found out. I missed the field, the world I had been in two hours ago. It had just imploded, sending life's shrapnel right back at me. For once, I could say, without a trace of melodrama, that my life might actually be over.

## Chapter Twenty-Seven

The shouting unfolded that night, long after Laurie had gone to bed. It wasn't as civil as I had hoped for and just kept getting more and more heated. I wanted to barge out and start telling my mother off as soon as she started blaming my father, yelling that he should have woken her up, or stood up to me. She called him things I hoped she didn't mean, and he did the same to a lesser degree. Tension and anger was seeping through every crack and crevice in the house, threatening to fill it up and drown us all.

I made my escape, throwing on a pair of slippers, and easing my window open. It was only a short drop down, enough to get out, but hard to get back in. I jumped up enough to pull the window shut, and slipped off through the yard, to the house next door. I unlocked the gate, and petted the dog, trying to make a quiet retreat to the window at Will's room. Camile thankfully stayed quiet, softly grunting with concern as she nosed my pockets and tried to lick my fingers. I knocked softly, and flattened against the house, one hand busy rubbing the shepherd's massive head to placate her.

Brian opened it, "Abby?"

"Some guard dog you have." I tried to force a very quiet laugh, and scratched the dog's ears, pleading for her to calm down and stop whining for affection.

"Will, it's your girlfriend."

"She's not my- Wait, Abby?" He stuck his head out, less than delicately shoving Brian out of the way.

"Can we talk?"

"The front door is that way."

"It's late."

"So it's so much less suspicious to climb in the side window. Great planning, Abs."

"Just help me...in you...idiot!" I grappled for the windowsill and tried to pull myself in. Will pulled back, struggling, and Brian hefted me in with one firm tug.

"You, couch." Will pointed to his brother, then the door.

"Wait, why?"

"For putting up with three years of Chad. Now, couch." He said again firmly and pointing animatedly at the door. I shot Brian an apologetic look from behind Will, and he left, shutting the door very quietly behind him.

"What's going on that's such a big deal that you're breaking and entering?"

"I'm not breaking and entering, you helped me in, remember?" I sat on Brian's bed, the only flat surface in the room that wasn't Will's.

"I'm expelled."

He cursed, profusely, running the range from angry to shocked to apologetic, entirely in the form of unprintable language, while gesturing with his good arm.

"My thoughts exactly." And I sighed and leaned back on the wall.

"Wow, that, wow. I'm so sorry Abs. That's screwed up."

"I'm not "expelled expelled" just strongly encouraged to never return, ever."

"So you could go back if you really wanted to."

"Do you honestly think I'd really want to? I don't need carrot bruises either."

He winced, and nodded, "They'll probably try to stone you, or go full Salem on you."

It was my turn to wince. "So, I'm sunk. My life is utterly over, at least the one I had."

"Are you going to go to a new school or what? Maybe we can go to Saint Something or Other's academy together."

"I don't know yet. My mom just found out half an hour ago, they were still yelling about it in the kitchen when I left."

"What's there to yell about? It's not your fault."

"I don't know. My mom yells when she doesn't know how to handle things, she's only scary and quiet when she thinks she has control over the situation. She goes from yelling to quiet to yelling again."

"Your poor dad."

"Yeah, I know…" I didn't really know exactly what was going on, but he was always on my side in things. Even when he wasn't, I saw him as the voice of quiet reason. I flopped, stealing Brian's bed. It probably should have felt a little weird to me, but it was my favorite perch when we played old consoles together at his house.

"So you came to get out of the angst-storm?"

"Yeah, I guess. It was just too negative, the vibes were all chaotic and it was ruining the feeling of the world, you know?" I'd tapered my voice into an old hippy's ramble.

Will laughed. "Bad vibes, man."

"Dude, exactly…" I nodded slowly and knowingly.

"Just keep it down, and use the bathroom off the kitchen. My parents would have a lot of weird questions for us both."

"Sure, that works. Can I stick around?"

"I take great pleasure in inflicting sofa revenge on my brother. I hate that thing, it smells like the dog."

I laid back, and stared at the ceiling. "If I tell you something weird, promise not to flip out?" I didn't look at him, just stared at the ceiling. That feeling had not been quiet since I'd come to the full realization, and it was clawing away at me.

"You're a dyke?" He asked, not seeming surprised, at all. "Abby I knew that."

"I'm not a lesbian."

"It's cool if you're—"

"I'm bisexual damn it."

"Half-lesbian?"

I rubbed my temples, palm wrapped around my face. "That's not what I'm trying to tell you, dumb-ass." I took a breath. "I'm transgender."

He was quiet a long moment. I resisted the urge to glance over; I didn't want to see his face right now. My body tensed, and I held back the urge to apologize. I tried not to cry, or panic, or do any of the great number of things that were suddenly trying to pop out of me. Damned emotions.

"So you are a lesbian."

"No, I want to be a boy, and I like boys and girls."

"Oh…damn, I had money on lesbian."

"Wait, what?"

"Kidding. I know what a transsexual is; I've used the internet a time or two."

A, long, awkward silence followed, my head now filled with less than enticing images of I'd run across in pop-up ads. I shuddered.

"Were-forums, you pervert. There's a few people on there who are, you know, like that," he added.

"So you're not freaked out?"

"Kind of confused, well, kind of. I mean, I can see that." He paused, "Definitely, but it's going to take some getting used to, you know? It's kind of a big deal. I mean, are you actually going to do everything?"

"I don't know yet. I mean, I want to do some things." It certainly sounded like he'd hung around the internet, but I was thankful he knew a little. "I just want to be a guy, you know? I don't know what

I'm clipping or keeping, I only just started reading into my options, you know?"

"Sure, whatever works. Can I call you Abby?"

"I guess. I kind of like Aaron."

"Are you going to freak out and yell at me if I call you Abby?"

"Nah. I'm not going to be an asshole about it. Frankly, I'm glad you aren't throwing consoles at me and telling me to get out your window."

"I'm not an ass." He said simply. "Besides, I'm glad you told me."

"Really?"

"Yeah, more teasing ammo."

"Jerk."

"This is how guys socialize, learn it." He glanced at the clock, and started to undress. I sat there like an idiot, not sure what I should be questioning, but pretty sure there was something. He pulled off his shirt, and britches, and climbed back into his own bed in his blue plaid boxer shorts. "I gotta be up in five hours. Night Ab- Er, Aaron."

"I can stay?"

"Sure."

"Really?"

"Shut up and go to bed or go home." He grumbled, and was almost instantly out cold, still mid-grapple with his pillow.

## Chapter Twenty-Eight

I slipped out early after Will had gotten up. I returned to my home, scurrying through the dew covered grass and back through the unopened garage-side door. I made it to my room without incident, and realized my hands were shaking, heart pounding in every appendage. I had gotten away with it.

I lay back on my own bed, wondering if I should steal another hour or so's sleep. I'd never realized just how early Will was up every morning, over an hour before I ever heard him go out and start tinkering. I reached for my phone. Something had been bothering me this last week and a half. I had never responded to Sylvia. She had sent me a few texts since, offering support, then apologizing, then just telling me how things had gone so far with her, and Brynn, just reaching out to me for some kind of response. I picked up the phone, and sent a simple, three word text.

**[You were right.}**

My phone didn't make a peep until my psychiatrist's meeting that afternoon. I sat in the waiting area with a programming magazine, forcing myself to be more genuinely interested in something for once. I waded through two paragraphs on HTML5 before I started to become genuinely interested, and it all started to come back to me again.

**{Are you mad?]**

**[No, just didn't want to admit it. Sorry I was a jerk.}**

**{It's all right. Was worried :( ]**

**[I'm sorry.}**

**{Sokay! :D]**

I assumed that must have meant it's okay, but I wasn't quite sure. It seemed to work, anyway.

**{Can I spam you with Easter Brynn pics?]**
**[K!}**

The wait was filled with photos of my cousin's daughter. I found some of them cute, some very cute, and some silly, but more than anything, I appreciated that Syl was talking to me again.

I was called back into Dr. Calhoun's office, and for once, she didn't have to ask me nearly as many questions. I explained everything, without inhibition, and almost without remembering to breathe. I found myself gasping for breath at the end of long and winding paragraphs, as I told her everything from what Syl said, to my meeting with Lilly, to being an ass to Lilly, to meeting with her again and explaining everything on her front yard, even to my coming out to William, and his complete coolness with it.

"That's quite a week." She nodded slowly, still catching up as she wrote. "I'm glad Lilly was helpful to you."

"She reminds me of a parakeet."

"She's definitely a bit like one, but she is quite knowledgeable."

"Parakeets can be smart." I shrugged.

"So, you're more sure of your identity now?"

I paused, and took a deep breath "It's…a lot to come to terms with, and I really don't want to be like this, I never have. But I don't know what to do, and it seems to work."

"I have some more worksheets for you to do, to help assess yourself better. I'll also be shifting the focus of our talks a little bit more towards dealing with your gender dysphoria. I've honestly not found anything else that needs addressed with higher priority."

I nodded slowly.

"And once you're comfortable, I would like you to start full-time experience. I find that that's one of the best ways to really assess yourself. Assuming you're ready to talk to your parents about this."

"Full-time experience?"

"To start dressing and interacting as male. Start using your preferred name and pronouns, and learning the mannerisms. Basically, start living as a boy." I looked skeptical, and she continued, "The experiences you have while doing this can be some of the best to gauge if this is really the right path for you. I find that while you can soul-search all you wish, there's a certain sense of commitment in actually starting the process. If you find yourself to be to averse to it, then we need to start considering other routes of treatment."

"That sounds…huge and terrifying." I nodded.

"It might be, but you'll probably find some relief from your symptoms. And you don't have to start until you're ready."

I sat in the man-eating chair, mildly terrified, and sure that I would never be any semblance of ready. I timidly asked, "And what would the first step be?"

"Telling your parents."

I smiled, and nodded, and knew that was never going to happen.

## Chapter Twenty-Nine

The never of a week ago, had dug itself into my brain. It itched, and it demanded, and there was no way to shut it up now. I had Dr. Cal's blessing, and Lilly's support, and the big road block in the way was just me. I lay back, and ignored the toolbox rattling out in my neighbor's driveway. Dad was up, something was sizzling, and mulling spices were in the air. It was probably more oatmeal, disguised as apples. I sat up, just enough to see Mom's car in the drive, and flopped back into the pillows. She was asleep, he was up, it was a weekend. Laurie would be in bed as late as Dad would let him sleep, and Dad didn't have work, there wouldn't have been a more perfect time, but was it worth it? Was happiness worth strife? Was I even sure? Was I just being a wimp?

I pulled out my phone, and sent a message to Syl.

**[Tell Dad, Y/N?}**

**{Why not?]**

**[I'm terrified.}**

**{Is that all?]**

I gave my phone a good, hard glaring and hoped I interrupted her aura.

**{ Scaredy Cat.]**

**[He could disown me!}**

**{He's your dad and he loves you! I'd be scared of your mom, not him.]**

Shit, she had a point.

**{He'll love you no matter what, Abby.]**

**[And Mom?}**

**{If she freaks, run. Or call me, I'll come get you.]**

**[That's-} I didn't drive, I had no idea how far off Syl was [A lot of gas}**

**{Worth it for my favorite cousin!]**

**[Thanks Syl. Should I do it now?}**

**{No time like the present]**

**[If I die, I blame you.}**

**{K.] Heartless, truly heartless.**

**{Tell me how it goes.] Slightly less heartless.**

I dressed in a hurry, and slipped out as quietly as possible. I had never woken Mom up by leaving my room before, but I didn't want to take any chances this morning.

"Morning, Pumpkin."

"What's for breakfast?" Suddenly even the barest of small talk just fell out of my mouth without a hint of grace. I stumbled, and sat down. Acting normal was a whole new game when I didn't even know what normal was to begin with. My heart was flopping around in my chest like a beached fish. There were two options at the moment, tell him, or pass out, and I wasn't sure which would be less traumatic. I took deep, relaxing breaths, while shaking and staring at the table top.

"Apple spice oatmeal."

"What?" I'd forgot I'd asked him a question. "Oh! Oh, good, good. Um, can we… talk?"

"Is everything okay, honey?"

"Yeah, yeah, no. No not quite."

"Is it about school?"

"Kind of."

"Well don't worry, your mother and I have been looking into alternative options." He said that with a worrying kind of fake cheer that screamed at me to not ask any more about this, possibly because he had no idea either.

"No, it's not school."

"But you just—"

I stared through the wood grain of the table, watching the swirls of pine. Deep, cleansing, terrifying breaths. I should have written a letter, that's what they suggested online, but no, I had to tell him in person. Past me had been a real dumb ass about this.

"So what is it?" His worried eyes settled on me, looking over the breakfast nook.

"I've been talking with Dr. Calhoun…"

He just looked at me, waiting for me to go on. Even the softest gaze was beating me over the head with guilt.

"And she thinks, I think…we think I might be…"

Another heavy pause, clouding up the room, filling our auras with slate blue dread. My eyes clenched shut, and I blurted it all out,

"I think I'm transgender!"

The storm of blue choked me out, and I hid in my arms against the table. I clung to it, for stability, for support, and waited for the world to fall in. The clouds around me went black, then grey, and swirled, cutting me off. I was alone on this island I'd made for myself, and all because I had the audacity to want to get better. It was over. Everything was over.

"Pumpkin?" A quivering voice in the storm. Something warm found me, and it took a long, hazy moment to realize I was being held. He hugged me close, and I looked up into a face that wasn't the anger I had braced for. "Abby, it's okay…"

## Chapter Thirty

They were still arguing. I could hear them in the kitchen, radiating a pulsing, erratic aura as things escalated and collapsed in waves. I couldn't feel one emotion, it was a jumble of everything I had ever read, everything except joy. The psychic hurricane was raging just down the hall, my mother's panic and loss, against my father's concern and sorrow. I threw myself back on the bed, watching a ragged, dripping calligraphy of numbers try to form in my head. They shook, lines quaking and paint spattering, as the invisible hand moved like it had been set on fire. The death throes of twenty-nine pulled me back into the world. There was no way out of this storm. I couldn't stay here, not tonight. My mother screamed, and it sliced through me, "Well sorry for thinking she was normal!" It was the crackle of thunder, and I heard all hell break loose down the hall.

I had left him to the wolves, I couldn't tell Mom, not on my own. He took the bullet for me, and for a whole day, we pretended nothing was wrong. Once Laurie was in bed, he made the move I couldn't, and I felt the aftershock from here. It had been two hours of black, thundering, screaming pain, and it was all my fault.

I took Syl's advice, and I ran.

I stuffed my clothes into my satchel, and eased my way out the window. I couldn't stay here tonight, not after that. They hated me now. As I rounded the corner towards the garage, I could still hear them fighting inside. My mother's aura had run out of rage, and I could see her slumped in her chair, head in hand. She was at a loss.

I looked across the way to my other home and wished I could kick Brian to the couch again. I needed someone. But, I knew they'd look for me at Will's. There was only one place left to go tonight. I slipped into the garage through the back, moving unnoticed past the kitchen window, and grabbed the old shop broom.

"Please don't kill me. Be good, just this once." I braced myself, ran forward, and kicked off. It shot off under me, and I clung to keep my grip. I yelped as I was hurled up, higher and higher. It tried to roll, and I clung fast and just let it until it evened out. It had its own issues, I had mine, or rather, it was fighting back against me, everything I had felt was coming out, and it wanted to tear me off. It was beyond my control, and there was only one thing I could go. I let my broom have its tantrum. The city lights whirled and blurred together below, headlights and taillights streaking like comets. I came at a near miss to a building; the rough brick surface seized my satchel and tore off the clasp. Then, it shot straight up.

"Do what you want!" I held on, clearing my mind as I was thrown about on the wind.

But then, it stopped, and hovered.

My knuckles were white and aching, and it stung to loosen my grip. I looked down hesitantly, and gasped, re-tightened my grasp. Hartford glowed in the distance, and far below, I watched Vernon twinkle. I exhaled, and leaned forward, letting the broom take me down. I dipped, and flattened myself against the surface as I flew past the river the wound through the silk mill, and shot through the tunnel, my shoes skimming the surface. Ever shifting webs of water reflected off the surface of the tunnel, catching the light and scattering across the ancient brick. I dipped my, fingertips into the stream that once cooled the mill, and savored the stark, cold sensation. I was invincible and devastated all at once, being flooded with the kind of courage I only knew after my world had ended. What was the worst that could happen now? Lights flashed in my face and someone laid on the horn just in time for me to dodge, and my new found confidence was knocked out of me. If I wanted to get there in one piece, I had to be calm, and I had to be careful. I kept over the woods, but followed the roads. I was sure someone would spot me; I wasn't sure how anyone on the highway could have missed a low flying witch. It was thankfully only a crescent moon, and I was dressed in dark clothing.

The calm of earlier was wearing off, as my Zen was being dampened by the cold and mist. The journey didn't feel magical anymore, and I would have killed to just have a car, to be riding along with Will or Lilly. My heart sank, and so did my elevation. I gasped, and leaned back as I struggled to keep it aloft. I had to hold myself together and not give in to any one feeling.

Could I really just go back home tomorrow? Would I have anywhere to go?

The broom dropped out from under me, and I clung, forcing it to pull up. "Oh Fuck!" I leaned back sharply, and it shot upwards. It bobbed. I held on for my life. I tried to steady it, flying towards the little town in the distance. My only safety was just three miles off in the distance. It was cold, and those three miles were the slowest in my life. I was buffeted by a gust of wind, and dropped again. "Please stay up…you can do it." I begged and pleaded with my broom, I didn't have the nerve to do it with myself. I'd ruined everything, just because I couldn't force myself to be something I wasn't. I should have stayed a girl; I shouldn't have bothered trying to change it all.

With the end in sight, every feeling I had known hit, at once, and I dropped out of the sky. I hit her front yard, literally, head and knees first. I landed sprawled, clumped with grass and mud. I looked back, and looked back at the broomstick embedded in the dirt, bristles waving faintly in the light wind. Well, I was alive at least. I hadn't even stood up when I was suddenly being hugged, and falling back into the mud. "Oh Aaron are you okay?"

"Yeah, no, Can we talk? Over tea?" I was developing a taste for it over the last month. We went inside, and I told her everything.

## Chapter Thirty-One

I woke when I always did; the sun had just peeked above the horizon. I waited to hear Will roll out with his clanking and rattling toolbox and start fiddling with a vehicle, or take an early morning ride of the world's fastest weed whacker. Instead I heard birds, and not a whisper or murmur of my neighbor or suburbia. I sat up, and looked over. Lilly was asleep to my other side, with a wall of pillows in between us as a divider. I didn't need it anyway, anything ungentlemanly had been the last thing on my mind. I sighed, and rolled onto my back, and stared up at the glow in the dark stars on her ceiling.

I wasn't sure where I could go now, and I waited for dawn to unfold, in a new and strange place.

"You awake?" Lilly mumbled, glancing over at me, her voice gravely and groggy.

"Sorry, force of habit."

"No, it's okay…want breakfast?" She sat up and fumbled for her glasses.

"If you want…" I didn't sound enthused. Even the idea of bacon couldn't quite lift my spirits right now. I climbed out of bed, and shuffled off to go change. I was wearing part of what I'd worn the night before, and a pair of Lilly's pajama pants with smiling little neon frogs all over it. Not my taste, but I was in no position to be picky while sobbing at three in the morning. I stuffed my old clothes in my satchel, and felt something hard in my pants pocket. I fished my phone out of my pants, light flashing. I had a missed three calls. Lilly was in the kitchen, still in her pajamas, and I ducked into the hall to listen.

When she peeked in to check on me, I was sitting on the floor, face in my hand.

"What's going on?"

"I need to get going, They're freaking out. They think I ran away." I didn't plan for that to happen. I guess I hadn't really planned anything.

"Need a ride?"

We sat in my kitchen, a mug of tea in everyone's hands. Lilly sipped and smiled faintly, her whole presence radiated warmth. I couldn't look at my dad, not even when he answered the door. He had aged overnight, and the harsh morning sun through the kitchen window highlighted grey hairs I had never noticed before. He looked exhausted, and clearly concerned. My mother said nothing, she was tense and drawn up, and watching Lilly critically. She was the barrier between my mother and I, as I sat at the bar-top nook, cradling a mug of tea, and for once savoring it, even if I found no comfort. The air smelled of stale sage, no doubt from my mother's stress ritual of the night before.

"Did you call the police?" I asked, which didn't seem like it was the smartest question in retrospect. Stupid conversation seemed better than silence.

"No, we thought you were with William, and not—"

"Oh, hi, I'm Lilly; I'm a friend of Aaron's." She smiled.

My mother did not, instead, she looked my way. "Are you sure? Aren't you just stressed? Being a teenager is hard, I mean, you don't have to be girly, and that doesn't mean you're a—" She couldn't say it.

"I know, but I don't think I can keep going, like I was. I've talked with Dr. Calhoun, and she said—"

"Are you sure she really said that you should do this?"

I sighed, "She said I should do what I feel like I need to do, to really figure out what's best for me. And I need to do this, I need to try it out, and know for sure."

"But you're so young, Just give it a few years and—"

"Ellie, I think we need to let Abby try what she thinks is best, and try to support her where we can, wherever this goes." My father looked my way, "You've always been responsible, and…I'm going to try to trust you, that this will be best for you. We'll love you, Abby, no matter what happens, you know that, right?"

The night before, I hadn't been so sure. I didn't know if I'd have a home to go back to. My mother stayed quiet, staring into the depths of her teacup. Her aura was a soft rain on a foggy evening, lost, and wavering. She wasn't angry at me, she was scared, and I was scared too. I wanted wrap her in a hug; I wanted to light the sage and bring her another mug of tea, but it was a distance I couldn't leap myself. She stayed quiet, while I answered Dad's questions, and Lilly did her best to reassure him. She was like me, and she had a job, friends, and went to college just like any other eighteen year old. She was normal. She was more normal than I had ever been.

Life tried to resume as usual when Laurie woke up, my father made breakfast, my mother went to bed. The house was quiet, but the storm clouds of the night before were slowly being blown away, as the familiarity of life started to settle back in.

"You're tall and beautiful ma'am." My little brother said to the silver-and-blue-clad waif of a witch at our kitchen table.

"Thanks honey." She smiled at him. I was almost jealous of the little twerp; he was a better flirt than I was.

## Chapter Thirty-Two

I woke with the sound of the toolbox going down the driveway, the morning ritual. The birds chirped outside, and I dragged myself out of bed before the rest of the world woke up. I didn't bother with the mirror, and dressed. The ritual had changed in recent weeks, sort of. Boxer-briefs, cargo pants, binder, shirt. I grabbed my helmet, and my leather jacket off the hook.

"Morning."

"It has been for ages, you know. Over an hour." And yet the rest of the world had yet to wake up.

"So how's saint who-what-now's?" I asked, leaning on the hood of my mother's car, which was parked in Will's driveway.

"It's St. Eustace's, and it's... like uniforms." Will sighed. "It's better than public school, anyway. And I'm as popular as always I'll have you know. But it looks nice on an application and no one has harassed me about being a rabbit."

"But unfortunately, you're still William the dork, eh?"

"Oh shut it. Do I need to start asking about your private life?"

"Like that would stop you anyway. Met any cute girls?"

"No."

"Boys?" I grinned, but a small part of me held out a little hope. It ran in the family, after all.

"You're a nuisance, you know that?" he grumbled, scooting back under the Outback. "Pass me the 6/19ths socket. It's over that way." He gestured, or rather, flapped his arm around while sticking out from under a bumper. I sighed, contemplating moving, and reached out gesturing in the air. I took a breath, and focused. The socket dragged itself over the toolbox lip, and skittered across the pavement. It plinked him in the arm. There was a thunk, and Will came scrambling out.

"Did you really just?" He was grinned like a maniac. I smirked, gestured, and hit him with a small wrench. "That's brilliant you stupid bastard!" I cackled.

"I can get Laurie's stuff off the roof now." I smirked, smug.

"Brian will be disappointed, you know, that was his job."

"Hey, I can reach tall stuff, and open jars now."

"Good for you, you're coming along nicely." He scooted back out, and smacked the bumper. "There, now don't break it again." My mother had finally caved and let him fix it.

"Only because you asked nicely. So… can we…?" I arched my eyebrows suggestively.

Will grinned, "Thought you'd never ask, but you know, I don't do this for most guys." He fired up the world's fastest weed whacker and grabbed his helmet.

"You're going to let me ride with you still? Isn't that gay?" I teased.

He shrugged, "Nothing wrong with that, and I'm not, by the way. Besides, it's a Vespa, there's only so much manliness I can claim to have. It's European, and so is sharing a ride."

"Thanks." I slipped on behind him, and buckled on my helmet. I tapped his leg, and we zoomed off. I kept a little distance, hands on his hips. I watched the world fly by around me. The grass was starting to brighten, and flecks of green were popping out of the dead, once barren trees that surrounded us. The bleak world of winter was giving way to spring, and the world was caught up in the middle of change. I was coming to terms with my own. At least, I had somewhere to go, and someone to drag along with me. Things might just be all right, and maybe the world wasn't quite as over as I thought it was. Will gunned the engine through the corner. I yelped and clung, hugging onto the back of him.

"Hey now."

"Shut up, hugging."

"Pick a side of the fence!" He laughed.

"Quiet, bunny boy."

"Jerk."

"Pansy."

"Did you honestly call me a pansy? You're the one who used to be a girl!"

"So? I'm still learning."

"Then stop hugging!"

We flung insults even when we could barely hear each other, and I stubbornly held on to my best friend, gender nonsense be damned. I was leaving the world of broomsticks behind, but as we shot through the corners, and overlooked the sprawling valley. It was in the first glow of dawn that I found a new way to fly.

## About the Author

Julian Norwood is a writer and illustrator living in rural Connecticut with his spouse, two cats, and a small menagerie of pocket pets.

Originally from Kettering Ohio, he has a degree in Studio Art from Defiance College, and finished his first children's book, *Up and Away*, as his capstone project. His first novel, *Forsaking Magic*, followed in 2014. He's been busy on an alphabet book for pre-schoolers, and more YA fantasy ventures, including the sequel for *Forsaking Magic*, and "Ambrose and the Cat."

Most of his work is painted, in various media such as casein and oils, and most of his writing is done at much too early in the morning.

When he's not writing, he's elbows deep in an engine, bottling the next home-brew project, enjoying a cup of tea, or traveling the countryside.

If you like Forsaking Magic, we suggest these books for you:

Red Kicks by jerjonji: http://www.wordbranch.com/red-kicks.html

The Sad Artist and Other Fairytales by Ndiritu Wahome:
http://www.wordbranch.com/the-sad-artist-and-other-fairytales.html

Dark Dreams by Christina Gray: http://www.wordbranch.com/dark-dreams.html

For a limited time get a 10% discount on any book purchased from the Word Branch Publishing Book Shop. Enter the code **CD10** at checkout. Start shopping here: http://www.wordbranch.com/book-shop.html

You can email Julian with your questions and comments at juliannorwood@wordbranch.com.

If you liked *Forsaking Magic*, please leave feedback.

*Forsaking Magic* is published by Word Branch Publishing, an independent publisher located in Marble, North Carolina. If you have a finished, or near-finished, book, we would like to hear about it. Word Branch Publishing believes that everyone has something important to say. http://wordbranch.com

www.ingramcontent.com/pod-product-compliance
Lightning Source LLC
Chambersburg PA
CBHW070014260626
47159CB00005B/1802

* 9 7 8 0 6 9 2 2 0 9 1 3 4 *